ROUGH RIDE

POWERTOOLS: HOT RIDES, BOOK #5

JAYNE RYLON

HAPPY ENDINGS PUBLISHING

V3

eBook ISBN: 978-1-947093-09-6

Print ISBN: 978-1-947093-10-2

Cover Design by Jayne Rylon

Cover Image by Wander Aguiar

Editing by Mackenzie Walton

Proofreading by Fedora Chen

Formatting by Jayne Rylon

ABOUT THE BOOK

Sevan has been keeping secrets. She's not the errand boy everyone at the Wildfire outlaw motorcycle gang thinks she is. No, she's been playing a dangerous game, hunting their president from inside their ranks in the name of revenge. And if anyone finds out, they won't hesitate to kill her.

Levi Jansen has always been drawn to Sevan, even when he thought she was a scrawny male mechanic named Rivet. He can't blame her for that since he's been hiding plenty too. As an undercover agent, he's relied on his tenuous partnership with ex-con, Ransom, to infiltrate Wildfire and build an ironclad case against them.

As the three of them swirl deeper into darkness, they'll need to rely on each other to find their way out, and back home to Hot Rides. Otherwise they're doomed to become exactly what they've been fighting so hard to defeat.

Allowing themselves to be distracted by desire would be the stupidest thing they could do. Unfortunately, it's impossible to ignore the sizzling attraction between them, complicating everything.

This is a standalone book in the Hot Rides series and includes an HEA with no cheating. The series is part of the greater universe where both the Powertools and Hot Rods books are also set, so you can visit with many of your previous favorite characters and see what they're up to now!

ADDITIONAL INFORMATION

Sign up for the Naughty News for contests, release updates, news, appearance information, sneak peek excerpts, reading-themed apparel deals, and more. www.jaynerylon.com/newsletter

Shop for autographed books, reading-themed apparel, goodies, and more www.jaynerylon.com/shop

A complete list of Jayne's books can be found at www.jaynerylon.com/books

1

S evan watched herself disappear. The makeup she'd worn swirled around the drain of a fancy marble sink, leaving her bare-faced and exposed. Without the wig she'd ripped off moments before and the acrylic nails she sheared from her fingers one by one with her pocketknife, she was transforming back into her alter-ego, Rivet.

Rivet was a puny prospect in the Wildfire outlaw motorcycle gang. Someone with a fresh mouth who was the least threatening and most easily overlooked in the pack, exactly as had suited her purposes. Oh yeah, Rivet was also a guy. At least that's what the assholes in the club thought, since women weren't allowed to join in their biker games.

She'd done her best to erase any traces of her femininity, although she'd never been especially girly, and had played into their biases. They didn't think a woman could know her way around engines better than they did. And Sevan was a killer mechanic.

Her grandfather had made sure of it. Only he

probably hadn't intended for this to be how she employed the skills he'd taught her over the years.

Too bad. This was what she had to do.

For herself.

For her murdered mother.

And for her half-sister—Joy—who'd only discovered Sevan existed a few minutes ago. The other woman had been so gracious and so welcoming that for a heartbeat, Sevan had felt her resolve weakening and her rage sputtering like an engine running out of gas.

What would it be like if she could forget her purpose and walk away?

Start a peaceful life here, in Middletown, with her sister—who'd previously been a friend even when she hadn't known they were related—Joy's new family, and the other skilled mechanics who owned and ran the Hot Rides motorcycle shop?

There was no use in dreaming about it because it wasn't going to happen.

Not until she made Angus—Wildfire's president—pay for what he'd done to her family and so many other people like them. At least she finally had some help.

Sevan swept her discarded claws from the counter into the pristine trashcan of country star Kason Cox's mountain lodge, so different from where she'd been and where she was heading. She couldn't allow herself to get used to any of this. Not the clean, luxurious accommodations, the newfound allies surrounding her, and definitely not the way she'd let her guard down around them almost instantly.

Not if she wanted to survive the coming weeks.

Sevan allowed her true self to be swallowed up and locked away in a deep, dark part of her psyche while stepping back to admire her handiwork in the mirror over the sink. A few passes of her splayed hand through her shorn hair made it stand up in spikey disarray. Her eyes were cold and hard. Unrecognizable. Perfect.

Rivet was back in control.

If seeing that too-familiar boyish face made her stomach cramp, she ignored it. It was one of many things she would have to compartmentalize if she was going to succeed on her mission. Desire was another. She rubbed her hands over her chest, making sure no hint of her recently hardened nipples, too pronounced to belong to a young man, showed through her T-shirt.

Her new boss, Jordan—one of Kason Cox's two lovers, that lucky bastard—had promised to conjure up some binders for her pronto. She supposed super spies and their teams of "security consultants" had access to all sorts of resources she hadn't while attempting to bring down Wildfire on her own.

That was a plus, because being in close contact with one of his minions, Levi Jansen, was going to make keeping her libido under wraps a necessity. Of all the damn people in Wildfire to be an undercover agent, it had to be him, didn't it? Son of a bitch.

Although it could be that his good guy/bad boy status was one of the reasons she'd always found the man to be so fucking sexy. Sure, he was skirting some pretty fine lines, but if they had the same goal, she could live with that.

They'd just have to pretend that one time he'd cornered her in the clubhouse bathroom and rammed his tongue down her throat had never happened. Especially since he'd thought she was a dude when he'd done it.

Hopefully he wasn't pissed now that he knew she was actually a woman.

Rivet closed her eyes, drew a deep breath, and repeated to herself, "You can do this. You have to do this. For Mom. For Joy. For Gram and Gramps. For you. You can do this..."

Her mantra was interrupted by a rap on the cavernous bathroom's door.

"Rivet, you almost ready?" Levi called. "We should hit the road. The longer we stay, the more likely it is someone will realize where we went."

She took one last peek at her reflection to verify all traces of Sevan had been wiped away before crossing to the door and wrenching it open. Automatically, her voice dipped to the tone she used while playing her role. "Yeah. Let's go."

"You'd better say goodbye to your sister." Levi's voice was softer than she'd ever heard it before, both quiet and tender.

Fuck that. She couldn't resist him if he was going to be considerate and in touch with his emotions and all that shit. No way. She'd barely managed it when she thought he was a piece of shit criminal.

"I can handle my personal business." She crossed her arms, hoping to obscure any lingering effects he had on her body. "Don't be like the rest of those Wildfire fuckers. Don't treat me different now that you know I'm dick-free."

"About that..." He leaned in, bracing himself with one palm pressed flat against the wall beside her head, just like he had that day in the clubhouse. Rivet supposed she'd asked for it. Asked for him to treat her like he had before, when he'd assumed she was an up-and-coming one-percenter of the nation's most ruthless outlaw motorcycle gang. "You should know, I wanted a hell of a lot more from you than that shitty little peck."

Shitty? Fuck him. That had been the best kiss of her life.

He dipped his head, coming perilously close to brushing his mouth over hers, which would result in her devouring him like she'd craved doing every day since the first time they'd collided.

"Hell, I still do. Even more now that I know what you're made of." Levi stared into her eyes. It gave her time to admire how fucking blue his were up close. Those eyes, and his blond hair, made him noticeable from across a crowded room. No matter who else was around, the moment he entered, she was drawn to Levi.

Tall, lean, bold, and intelligent, he had no trouble revving her engines.

"Made of?" Rivet snorted. "You mean like tits and a vagina?"

"Nah." Levi grinned, slow and wide. "I don't have much preference when it comes to where I put my dick. But smart-mouthed, competent, and brave to the point of stupid...that's my type right there."

Rivet's breath caught as his praise penetrated deep within her, nearly reaching the place she'd caged her true self. Except fooling around with him would be the absolute worst thing she could do.

Apparently, his partner in this madness—an ex-con named Ransom—agreed with her.

"Levi! What the fuck did we just finish discussing?" He fisted the back of Levi's T-shirt in his meaty grip and hauled the other man a solid three feet away from her, as if Levi was as light as a distributor cap. "This shit will get us killed. Even if no one figures out Rivet isn't who he says he is, Wildfire isn't going to tolerate guys like us hanging around."

Us? Rivet's eyes widened. Did that mean Ransom and Levi were both into guys?

Or maybe even each other...

Holy. Shit. How had she missed that? Simple. Like he said, their secret was as damning as her own in the eyes of the motorcycle gang. Any slips would be a death sentence for the three of them. "We're screwed, aren't we?"

"Yes. Are you sure you don't want to stay here?" Levi barked as he rearranged his junk, making it even more obvious that he was hard and hung.

"Positive." And if Ransom hadn't shoehorned some distance between them, she would have been likely to have kneed him in the nuts for suggesting it. If he couldn't control himself, *he* should be the one to sit this assignment out.

Before she could tell him so, Levi turned to Ransom. "Hey, don't act like I didn't tell you it's going to be an issue. This is the worst plan we've ever had."

Had Levi been arguing against including her because of their attraction? That did a lot to douse her lust for him. "Don't you dare think you're leaving me behind. I've earned this. Put in my time, same as you."

Surprisingly, Ransom nodded. Where Levi was light, and wit, and patience, Ransom was everything else. Hair the color of aged whiskey and eyes to match, he was more about brawn than brains. She had never for one second doubted he was exactly what she'd thought—a full member of the club capable of brutality and enjoying it while he was at it.

Except at that moment, he seemed to be the only one thinking straight. "Yeah, this is personal to you, Rivet. I get that. But whatever is happening between you two...can't. I'm sorry."

"I'm not." She flicked her gaze to Levi, who was still staring at her mouth.

It didn't matter how damn handsome the man was—if he insulted her, she wouldn't tolerate that kind of bullshit. She wanted someone like the two men who had flanked her sister when she'd come clean about who she was and why she was there. Ones who would support her without taking away her freedom. Guys who would trust that she was strong enough to handle them both.

Both? When had the possibility of claiming more than one man occurred to her? Was it when she'd realized the mechanics of the Hot Rides motorcycle shop where her sister's boyfriends worked were as adventurous in bed as they were in their designs? Or when her sister had openly admitted she was simultaneously in a relationship with Angus's son Walker as well as Dane, his best friend? Or had it been in that instant when she'd so recently realized Levi and Ransom were partners both on the Wildfire case and outside of it?

It didn't matter. Because Ransom was right. They couldn't mess around. Not if they wanted to survive.

"I'll be out the door in five or less." Rivet marched between Levi and Ransom, leaving them gawking after her.

Low rumbles of their continuing disagreement reached her ears, though she couldn't distinguish the arguments they made to each other in her wake. So she returned to the living room where Joy paced as both of her boyfriends hovered protectively nearby. Dane cradled their infant daughter. His big hands looked so different when they clutched such a fragile being, prepared to protect it at any costs, than they had when he'd dipped his booted toe in the Wildfire arena. Walker and Dane had returned from overseas with the military only long enough to figure out that they had outgrown Angus's organization and his ever-degrading morals.

And long enough to knock up Joy, apparently.

Rivet smiled as she approached, but the expression must not have been any more reassuring to her audience than it was to herself. Joy bit her lower lip and Walker frowned. Even Jordan—the newly appointed head of whatever quasi-government black ops group had decided to back her, Levi, and Ransom—hesitated before he asked, "Are you sure you want to do this? You can still change your mind."

"Not going to happen." Rivet planted her feet and crossed her arms. She might not have the heft of Ransom or even Levi, but she was twice as determined to bring Angus and Wildfire to justice.

"Okay." Joy didn't try to talk her out of it. "But you remember this. We're counting on you coming back when this is finished."

"Thank you for saying that, but I could never afford my own place and I wouldn't expect to crash at yours." Her sister had an adorable tiny home on the Hot Rides property, along with most of the other people who worked there. The instant Rivet had caught a glimpse of it, when they'd whisked her to safety after confronting Wildfire's ex-sergeant-at-arms, she'd felt an indescribable heaviness. Like she never wanted to move from that place again. Not that she had a choice.

"I know it's nothing fancy like this." Joy smiled as she gestured at the mountain mansion Kason shared with

Jordan and their girlfriend Wren. "But we'd make room for you."

"And I will gladly vouch for your skills to Gavyn and Quinn, the owner and manager of the garage," Walker added. "You always were a kickass mechanic. We could use you at the shop. It wouldn't take long for you to earn your spot and work into a home of your own."

"There's a place for you here in Middletown," Dane agreed. "Work and family. You can have a good life here. Anytime you want it. Like right now."

"Tempting but...I can't." Rivet sighed. "I would never respect myself if I gave up now that there's a sliver of a chance I could actually do what I've been planning all this time."

Walker cursed under his breath. "I should have taken him out myself. He deserves it for what he's done to your... no, *our*...family."

"You could never have done that." Joy turned to him and smothered him in a hug. "Because you're nothing like your father and I wouldn't love you if you were."

No one mentioned that Walker's father had also been Joy's stepdad. The other woman didn't care about that fucker, who'd looked the other way when his sergeant-at-arms— Clive—had raped Joy right in Angus's own home in order to stake some sick claim on her. She did, however, care about Walker and making sure he lived a long, whole, happy life.

One not spent behind bars either.

"Don't worry, I've got you covered." Rivet smiled at Walker and hoped it wasn't as wolfish as it felt.

"I don't like this." He grumbled, "But it's not like I can stop you."

"Sure can't." Their concern was eroding her

confidence in her purpose. Rivet had to bail before they convinced her to abandon everything she'd been struggling to attain for years. "Thanks for everything. I gotta go..."

Damn if her eyes didn't burn then. Her throat constricted. What the fuck?

Rivet had conditioned herself not to feel, and certainly not to show it if she did. Mistakes like this would be the end of her at Wildfire. She'd stayed too long already. When she turned toward the exit, where she assume Levi and Ransom were waiting, Joy called to her.

"Wait. Sevan!" She rushed over to Rivet and squeezed her shoulders. "I have one other reason for you to make it back safe and soon."

She tipped her head like a curious dog. "Yeah?"

"My daughter Arden needs a godmother." Joy sniffled.

"Who? Me?" She would have stumbled back a step or two if Joy hadn't held her steady with a surprisingly strong grip.

"Of course. You're the only family I have." Joy hugged Rivet tight enough she might have cracked a rib or two.

"I beg to differ." Rivet looked over her shoulder at Walker, Dane, the baby, Jordan, and the photos of the rest of their Hot Rides family that littered the walls.

Joy didn't argue. Still, she pulled back and held Rivet at arm's length, leveling a decent mom-stare at her. It had been a long time—okay, maybe never—since Rivet had felt that combination of love and consternation.

"Don't give me any shit, little sister." Joy shook her a bit. "Get out of here now and make it back quickly. In one piece."

"I'll do my best." Rivet couldn't resist squashing Joy for a moment before she retreated first one step and then another. Before she turned her back, she said, "Thank you. All of you. But especially for asking me...that. I would love to be Arden's godmother."

"Done," Joy said with a smile that was echoed by Walker and Dane.

"Come on. I'll walk you out." Jordan came up beside them and ushered Rivet to the front door. It felt like he was delivering her from one bad situation, where she'd nearly been busted as a mole, into something more dangerous, where she was formally a spy and tangled up with Levi and Ransom to boot.

If she had any other options, she would take them. Unfortunately, she didn't.

2

———

Levi couldn't believe his luck. On the one hand, having Jordan and his newly formed team on their side, with the wealth of resources that came along with them... Well, shit, that was going to make some things much easier. Having to bring Rivet with them now that he knew the cute, misguided young man was really a gorgeous, avenging woman named Sevan...

Yeah, that was going to make some things, like his cock, a hell of a lot harder instead.

"Can you believe we work for this guy, now?" Ransom nudged Levi in the ribs with his elbow as he peered around the great room of the mountain lodge where Jordan had established his headquarters.

"Wonder what happened to the last guy." Levi wouldn't miss that bastard. Their handler had been a dweeby, by-the-books detective who had no idea how the dirty work needed to be done on a case like this. Jordan was a massive upgrade, even if it did mean they were now operating in some kind of legal gray area.

"Who knows, but..." Ransom cleared his throat. "You

sure this is legit? Are they going to keep their end of the deal with me when this is done? Or act like they don't know shit to cover their asses and send me back where I came from?"

Ah, fuck. Levi probably should have considered that possibility.

Whatever wrongs Ransom had committed to land him in the slammer, he'd earned a reprieve by risking his life to set things right. The guy might have his own slightly skewed moral code, but he'd never once let Levi down. He trusted Ransom with his life, every single moment of every single day, and not only when they were in the clubhouse—or in bed—together. "You want to wait until we get something in writing from Jordan? That they're going to let you walk, free and clear, after we're done?"

"What's the point? You know it don't work like that." Ransom stared up at the exposed-beam ceiling—way, way over their heads. Just like the level of the bullshit they were about to be slogging through again. "Even if he would leave an evidence trail like that, which he won't, it doesn't mean his bosses are going to honor the contract when we're finished."

"I'll do everything I can—"

"I know. It's just that sometimes that's not enough. I guess I'm going to have to take it on faith, and you know I'm not real good at that." Ransom scrubbed his hand over his mouth and close-cropped beard, making Levi wish they were alone so they could release their tension in much more pleasurable ways.

With Rivet around, even physical relief was likely to be denied to them. He couldn't say why exactly, but the thought of fooling around with Ransom while Rivet was in next room didn't sit right with Levi. Maybe because of how damn bad he wanted to do the same with him—or her, he reminded himself. She was a woman and would want to be thought of that way by anyone who knew her secret. It wasn't that she was living as a man because she identified as one, which he would respect if that was the case. Her ploy was a means to an end. If it weren't for Wildfire, she would go back to being the feminine beauty he'd gotten a glimpse of earlier.

He shifted as his dick started to twitch.

"Dude, I'm telling you shit I would rather not even think about myself and you're distracted? I know that look. You're thinking about sex. With Rivet." Ransom smacked Levi with the back of his hand. "What the hell kind of friend are you?"

Son of a bitch. "A terrible one. I suck. How many times do I have to tell you that before you'll believe me?"

Ransom grinned. "If we had a few more minutes, I'd drag you back to the bathroom and prove you right. Least you could do is blow me when I'm freaking out over here. Besides, you're not the only one who noticed how fucking hot Rivet was all dolled up, you know."

"Not. Helping." Levi arranged himself as he saw Jordan approaching with Rivet out of the corner of his eye. He was used to being hyperaware of his surroundings, but that wasn't why he homed in on her. It was always like that with Rivet. He could practically sense when she was in the room and what she was doing as if she was branded on his consciousness.

It had already been nearly impossible to stay away from her. Now it was going to be pure torture.

"You three set?" Jordan didn't look happy about sending them out on their own again. And to be honest, for the first time in a while, reluctance pulled at Levi. It was hard not to notice how fucking happy the Hot Rides folks were. Walker, Dane, and Joy looked like entirely new people now that they'd started fresh, and done it right.

Levi'd never imagined that he'd live long enough to get out of the undercover game. Hadn't really cared about it either. Maybe this would be his last mission for a while. If they survived it.

He was getting older and possibly a little soft. No one lasted past that.

Still, he wasn't about to let Ransom or Rivet do this without his support. They had to go back for their own reasons. That meant he had to return with them. If he did, maybe he could make up for some of his own transgressions. "Yeah. Let's do this."

"Sooner we leave, sooner you can come home," Ransom said to Rivet.

Levi was well aware that his partner didn't include himself in that vision of a rosy future.

The three of them were so screwed up.

Living a normal life seemed like an impossible dream. That didn't stop Levi from imagining it for a moment anyway. Him, and Ransom, and Rivet chilling out at this gorgeous lodge without fear of retaliation or their pasts haunting them. Working on their bikes or spending hours riding on the scenic, rural roads surrounding Middletown. Wind in their faces. Then, later, nights filled with their bodies tangled in sweaty sheets.

It sounded like heaven. Some sort of farfetched fantasy.

Unfortunately, for any of them to have a shot at something like that, even separately, they would first have to ride through hell. Together.

"I'm ready." Rivet stepped away from Jordan and closer

to Levi. It took every shred of willpower he had not to put his arm around her and draw her to his side. He had to remember what it would take to convince Wildfire that they were bonded by their patches and not by a common goal or their magnetic attraction to each other. He couldn't slip, not even for moment. So it was better not to get used to anything else now.

Besides, Rivet probably wouldn't appreciate his protectiveness anyway. She'd already shown she was capable of taking care of herself, even if he wanted to do it for her.

"So here's what you'll do," Jordan instructed. "Head toward Wildfire. Get far enough away from here that it's believable you escaped the cops when they crashed into the diner and arrested Clive. Say you saw Rivet's bike at a cheap roadside motel, so you stopped and picked him up on the way. Spend tonight there together. Then tomorrow go back in. Don't let yourselves get separated."

"Won't Angus be suspicious that Rivet's had a change of heart or that he was trying to defect when he reached out to Walker, Dane, and Joy?" Ransom crossed his arms. "I'm not going to hand him over just so Angus can make an example of him."

"No. We're already planting seeds. Walker sent his dear old dad some texts ranting that Angus's plan to get Joy back by sending Rivet here isn't going to work. Angus believes Rivet was trying to earn favor and prove he was worthy of being promoted to a full member by talking Joy into returning to Wildfire."

"As if." Rivet rolled her eyes, though it wasn't a bad line of reasoning, really. That's exactly the shit Angus's minions would pull. They were constantly jockeying for power even amongst themselves. It was one of the things that kept everyone in line—they couldn't trust anyone else in the gang even though they were supposed to be a band of brothers and all that idealistic bullshit.

Maybe some clubs were like that. But not Wildfire. Wildfire was rotten from the inside out.

"And you think he bought it?" Ransom wondered.

"Absolutely." Jordan seemed certain, which went a long way toward settling the churning in Levi's guts. "A president like him, one who's out of control—a tyrant—has come to think they're invincible. I doubt he'd believe someone like Rivet would dare to rebel. Especially not if you two back up Rivet's story. Angus respects you and has no reason to think you're anything but soldiers in his army."

"Which goes to prove that he can be fooled." Rivet nodded. "I'm willing to take the chance. Let's ride."

Did she have to say it like that? Levi smoldered, stuck between desire and fear, longing and repulsion. He hated what he'd become, the things he'd gotten snared in. This was the only way to put a stop to it once and for all.

He looked at Ransom, giving him the final say.

The other man nodded once. They were in.

Levi slapped him on the back. "Let's go."

3

————

Levi and Ransom parked on either side of Rivet's sleek graphite Honda CMX 500 Rebel. Their beefier, more traditional motorcycles dwarfed hers, though they weren't nearly as fine-tuned or customized. She'd done a lot of quality work to it. Stuff that had made the Hot Rides eager to offer her a place in their ranks should she decide to return to Middletown after this fiasco was finished.

Hopefully, she would take them up on the opportunity.

Levi had hated letting her get ahead far enough to make their staged reunion believable to anyone who might spot them rolling through town. Slowing down to ride side by side with Ransom as she flew past them then grew smaller and smaller in his sights had been one of the hardest things he'd had to do lately.

He suspected it would quickly lose its place on that list, though. The next few weeks, or months—however long it took—were going to be rough ones.

"Hurry up," Ransom growled as he swung his leg over his bike, then headed for the room closest to where Rivet had left her bike. In full view of the nearby highway, it was as obvious as the half-dead neon sign flickering over top of the probably roach-infested lodge. Grunge-colored wooden shingles were mostly intact, though dotted with moss, making the single-story building with external doorways look as if it had some kind of pox.

It was exactly the sort of place Wildfire would associate in. Hopefully no one else had found Rivet before they had. The light was on, though the curtains were drawn, and he couldn't hear anything from the other side of the flimsy door.

Ransom knocked on it, making the whole thing bend despite the fact that he hadn't hit it hard with his admittedly substantial fist. "Hey, Rivet. You in there?"

"Open up, asshole," Levi added so she'd know it was them and only them. "We know you're in there."

The sound of a chain, which wouldn't do much good to keep out anyone intent on entering, slipping off a metal plate was followed by crusty yellow light pouring onto the cracked sidewalk. Rivet looked them up and down before jerking her chin toward the interior of the room and turning her back on them.

That's when Levi realized what sort of night they were in for—the long, painful variety.

When he groaned, Ransom went on high alert. His partner crowded close. Ransom peered over Levi's shoulder as if expecting a welcoming party. He shouldn't have bothered. No Wildfire—or rival gang—members were waiting for them inside.

"What's wrong?" Ransom asked.

"There's only one fucking bed," Levi hissed. He cursed

under his breath as he went inside, Rivet leading the way and Ransom right behind him, sandwiching him between them. Ransom shut the door and locked them inside with a distinct *snick*.

"Sorry, this is all they had." Rivet crossed the tiny gap between the round table for two by the window and the saggy mattress. It was probably for the best he couldn't see more of the stained brown carpet than the strip in between the beat-up furniture.

She toed off her riding boots and settled onto the bed, sitting cross-legged, something she would never have done in the clubhouse. It reminded him that although she looked like Rivet, inside Sevan was still there with them.

It kind of freaked him out and turned him on at the same time.

"I don't get the feeling this is a family establishment with the need for multiple-bed rooms." Ransom shrugged.

Rivet cracked a smile at that. "Nah. More like a work zone for dealers and prostitutes. And outlaw motorcycle gang members. I'm kind of surprised we haven't had any business over this way before, to be honest. It's only thirty miles from the clubhouse."

She had that right. Levi nodded. "You did good. They'll find us here, sooner rather than later."

"Thanks." Rivet looked up at Levi and then Ransom. Was she having a change of heart? He realized her concern wasn't for herself but for them when she echoed his thoughts. "Last chance to bail, guys. Go now or get dragged in again. Don't stay on my account. I can handle it myself if you two aren't around."

"No fucking way." Ransom glared. "Don't insult me

like that. Besides, we're in this for our own reasons. Not only to watch your perky ass."

"Technically, it's my job." Though it had become so much more to him than an assignment. Levi knew the same wasn't true for her. For Rivet, this was entirely personal. "Unless I'm going to resign, I don't really have a choice."

"So quit." She looked at him like he was nuts. "This isn't worth a paycheck unless yours has a fuck-ton more zeros on it than mine does."

"Doubt it. But no. I'm going to see this through. You don't have to worry about that."

When her shoulders relaxed a hair, he knew he'd said the right thing.

"Me too." Ransom reassured her. Levi's honor might be on the line, but Ransom's freedom also hung in the balance. No, they were in this until the end.

But why was she so hell bent on causing Angus to fall?

"So how exactly did you get sucked into all this?" Levi leaned up against the wall with one shoulder, wincing internally at his use of the word *suck* again. He was going to have to eliminate it from his vocabulary for awhile.

When Ransom covered a snort with a cough, Levi knew the other guy had noticed too.

"Easy. Angus murdered my mom. And so far he's gotten away with it." Rivet plucked pills off the worn comforter and flung them onto the carpet. "No one should be able to do that."

"Shit! I'm sorry." Ransom looked like he might hyperventilate, or maybe puke. Of course he'd see all the similarities to his own sins and none of the differences. Levi was too far away to put his hand on his friend's back and the other guy probably wouldn't appreciate him doing it in front of their new partner anyway.

That didn't mean he didn't wish he could.

Levi hated to see his best friend—*only* friend—tormented. He feared every day that something might push him over the edge into self-loathing and self-harm. He'd have to keep a careful watch on Ransom. Even more vigilant than usual after Rivet unburdened herself to them.

"Your mom was Joy's mom too, right?" Levi asked. He'd heard some of what she and Jordan had been discussing at the mountain retreat, but not all the details. They could be critical to the case and how things played out back at the clubhouse. More importantly, though, he found himself wanting to know about how they impacted her. *Uh oh.*

"Yeah. Biologically speaking." Rivet toyed with the top edge of her sock. "She pretty much split on me, though. When she got back together with Angus, she forgot all about me. Left me with my grandparents, who raised me."

"What happened to her?" Ransom wondered, his voice more in line with that of a smoker or someone with bronchitis than his usual smooth bass. "I've heard whispers around the club, but most of them say Angus got a lot crueler after she passed away. We assumed that was part of what pushed him into this darker shit he's involved in these days."

"The sick part is, it might be. He could have loved her with some part of his shriveled black heart. That doesn't mean he could accept her. She was unfaithful to him. Or at least that's how he took it. He met her years ago, when Joy was five or six, but he was young and not real fond of commitment. Had a harem of whores at the clubhouse and no serious old lady. My mom wasn't a saint either. She had a lot of pride. So when he refused to favor her, she got fed up with it and walked."

"Even back then that had to have been rough. Angus isn't the kind of guy to give up without a fight." Ransom sank into the shitty chair closest to the window. When her story got too difficult for him, he would peer out the gap between the curtain and the edge as though they wouldn't hear the rumble of approaching motorcycles from a mile away.

Wildfire was not subtle.

"Yeah. From what I've heard, he never fully got over her leaving in the first place and tested her for years because he thought she wasn't as loyal as she should have been. Whether it was because she was the only person who ever said no to him or because he had some kind of affection for her, he had to have her. According to my grandparents, she never really got over him either. She was strong. Too much for a lot of guys, and even the ones who were interested couldn't challenge her. Especially not whoever it was that knocked her up with me. She never even told him I existed. Didn't want him hanging around. Refused to tell my grandparents who it was either."

"That's completely unfair." Levi couldn't imagine having a child and never knowing about it. No matter how Rivet idolized her mom and was willing to risk everything to make Angus pay for stealing her, he could see another side. The woman had been far from perfect. Then again, no one was. Not him. Not Ransom. And not even Rivet. That didn't mean anyone deserved to have their life snuffed out over it either.

"It is. To him and to me. It's not like I know who he is or could tell him even if I wanted to. Another thing Angus

24

took from me when he killed her, so add it to the list of reasons why I hate him." She punched the comforter beside her thigh.

"But when Joy's mom came to Wildfire and married Angus, she only had one daughter with her." Ransom scratched his chin.

"Yeah." Rivet tried not to show them her pain, but the flash of hurt and disappointment in her pretty eyes was hard to mask. "She never told him about me. Or the other guys she took for a test ride while she and Angus were broken up. Like I said, my grandparents raised me."

"Let me guess, they filled your head with stories of how amazing your mother was and how Angus corrupted her and how it was all his fault that your mom made bad decisions." Ransom didn't pull his punches.

Although he'd had the exact same thought, Levi glared at the other man for actually saying it out loud. Rivet wasn't ready to hear the truth. "Take it easy."

"It's okay. He's pretty much right." Rivet slumped further. "I thought of her as some kind of princess locked in an evil tower. So I tried to rescue her. One day when she was out shopping, I went up to her in a store at the mall and tried to tell her she could escape with me. That my grandparents were waiting in the car outside."

A knot of dread formed in Levi's gut.

"Oh shit." Ransom muttered.

"Yeah. That didn't go over well." Rivet put her face in her hands for a moment. "She freaked out and insisted that I leave, alone, but I wouldn't go. I grabbed her and started dragging her away. I didn't realize that as Angus rose in power to the presidency, that meant his old lady— the queen—would be guarded."

"Why would a normal girl have any idea about how an MC works?" Levi asked softly. "You couldn't have known."

"When they surrounded her and ripped me away to toss me out the storeroom door into the loading area behind the mall, I screamed for my mom not to leave me. Again." A tear escaped the corner of her eye and rolled down her cheek.

Levi knew better than to wipe it away no matter how badly his fingers ached to do so.

"When the club members reported back to Angus that my mom had another child, he put it all together. You know as well as I do, he doesn't keep people around that he doesn't believe are loyal. And certainly not ones that he is vulnerable to because he cares for them when he feels they've betrayed him." Rivet didn't seem to have the strength to finish, so Levi filled in the blanks for her.

"When I joined the club, I heard Joy's mom had died when she took Angus's bike out in the rain without his permission. That she was incompetent...."

"She wasn't! My grandfather had taught her how to ride when she was a kid. Hell, it was partly because of her abilities that she'd caught Angus eye in the first place when he brought his bike in to be fixed. She was trying to escape. She was going to come home." Rivet's fists balled against her slender thighs.

Levi held his hands up, palms out. "I believe you."

"Angus had her killed when she was trying to make her way back to you. Didn't he?" Ransom asked gently. It seemed odd coming from the big guy, but Levi felt his admiration for the other man grow when he handled the situation and Rivet so delicately.

"Clive bragged about it to me once. He did it, but Angus ordered it. Worse, it was my fault." Rivet bit her lip hard enough he was afraid her tooth was going to cut it open. "I got her killed. If it wasn't for me, she'd still be alive. Joy would still have her mom. Hell, she wasn't even really my mother. I hardly remember her. Only the stories my grandparents used to tell me. And when my Gram got sick, I hoped she could have her dying wish: to see my mom one more time. It was foolish."

"It was no one's fault but Angus's," Levi promised, though he knew Rivet wouldn't believe him. Those empty reassurances hadn't done anything to lessen his own guilt. When someone you loved was hurt—or worse—and you had something to do with it...well, that shit would fuck you up for life.

"Maybe, but I'm going to make it right. He's going to pay for what he did. And now there's even more at stake. The only person who's been able to wound him as deeply as my mom is Walker, his own son. Which is another reason I have to do this. I couldn't protect my mom, but I still have a chance to make sure my sister and her new family stay safe. Angus needs to be stopped once and for all, before he destroys more lives. Hopefully my mom would be able to forgive me and wouldn't have been too ashamed to say I was hers if I can do that."

Levi couldn't help himself. He settled next to her, put his hand over her crossed ankles, then squeezed, surprised at how slender her bones were. Rivet was badass, no doubt about that, but she seemed larger and tougher than she actually was. How much of that had been pure bravado? "She would never have blamed you in the first place."

"Damn straight." Ransom's mouth was set in a grim slash. "I've heard other stories about her. Besides, to have lived with Angus that long...she was tough. And shrewd. She knew what was up."

Neither of them mentioned that she might also have been vicious in her own right, a perfect pairing for the head of Wildfire. They let Rivet keep some of her memories untarnished.

She nodded, but didn't seem able to say any more than that.

After a few moments of awkward silence, Levi told her one of the few things that might help. "I always knew you were different. Better than the rest of those assholes in the club. I hope someday you come to realize it too."

No response to that. He made it a new goal to ensure that Rivet saw at least some of what he did when he looked at her before they were through.

Lost in thought, the three of them were quiet for a while. Until Rivet shifted, breaking Levi's hold on her legs. His hand felt empty without the contact, which had grounded him as well. It had been a long time since he'd had an entirely genuine connection with someone. Whatever it was he had with Ransom was tainted by their involvement in shady dealings and mutual desperation.

Another problem to work on, but did he want to? What would happen when they were done here? Would they go their separate ways? Neither of them was in a position to make promises about the future, nor likely to do so even if they could. Not after the things they'd lived through.

"What about you?" Rivet asked Ransom. "What are you doing here? Saving the world, like Levi?"

"Hell no." Ransom huffed out a mirthless chuckle. "I'm in this mess because it was my get-out-of-jail-free card."

"So that wasn't a cover story? You really are an ex-con?" Rivet leaned forward instead of recoiling. The woman had absolutely no sense of self-preservation. Couldn't she tell it was a touchy subject?

Maybe she didn't give a fuck after they'd prodded her own tender spots.

Her unflinching stare demanded answers.

4

"It ain't something I'm proud of." Ransom shifted his stare out the streaky window again so he didn't have to meet either Rivet or Levi's gazes directly as he confessed. Frankly, he hated admitting even that much. Prison, and the nightmare that had landed him there, wasn't exactly a topic he enjoyed discussing. "Not worth bragging about despite what the crowd at Wildfire assumes. You've been hanging around them too long if you think it is."

"Hey, I'm sorry." The impact Rivet's soft apology had on him shouldn't have been profound, yet it was. Especially combined with the light contact of her fingers on his forearm. She leaned forward until she was perched precariously at the edge of the bed.

In his peripheral vision, he saw Levi reach out again to steady her—as if he needed any excuse to touch her—as she bridged the narrow chasm between them. When was the last time someone had attached themselves to him like that? Not out of anger, or brutality, or even lust like Levi did sometimes, but pure compassion?

A long fucking time.

Ransom cleared his throat and tried not to let his guard down any more than it already was. Who was he kidding? He was wrapped around Rivet's little socket wrench.

The woman was fearless and had good intentions even if she made terrible decisions. She sort of reminded him of himself, before his life had gone to shit. And look where that had led him...to the underbelly of humanity.

Affection was a weakness none of them could afford.

"Don't worry about it." After a few moments, he shrugged her hand off, trying to scrub the sparks of desire she'd left behind from his awareness as easy as he'd dislodged her grip.

Good luck with that.

Ransom hadn't stopped thinking about what it would be like to kiss her since he'd walked in on Levi about to devour her in the lodge up at Lake Logan. He'd been jealous as fuck. Nearly as envious as the time Levi had admitted to doing the same to her right in the Wildfire clubhouse bathroom before they'd even known she was a she.

They'd been shitting themselves for a solid week after that incident, sure that Rivet would rat Levi out for being bisexual. Only thing was, she couldn't have done so without implicating herself at the same time. And even still, Ransom had secretly figured it would still have been worth it.

He sure as shit didn't blame Levi for the hard-on he had for the mechanical genius in their midst, even if it had been reckless to indulge it both then and again now.

Maybe he'd get over it if he evened the score.

His gaze flicked into the room, past Levi's curious blue

stare to Rivet. They gazed into each other's eyes, something weighty and intense passing between them. They each had their baggage. Had made choices that led to someone getting hurt, whether they meant to or not.

She understood and didn't judge him for his mistakes, at least not given what little she knew of his at the moment. The three of them made an oddly well-suited team. Coming to an unspoken understanding, they both shook their heads, as if surfacing from a dive into a warm lake in summer.

No. No, they definitely should not go any farther down that road.

Ransom stood up then, abruptly enough that his chair rocked onto its back legs. The rumbling of his stomach served as a perfect distraction. "I don't like the idea of any of us leaving by ourselves, but we gotta order a pizza or something. I'm starving."

Levi moaned, which didn't help Ransom's near-boner situation. He loved making the other man give in and express himself like that in the middle of the night. Though he hadn't ever imagined sleeping with a guy before he'd gone to prison, since then he'd learned the value of human contact regardless of a person's gender.

"That sounds like heaven." Levi rubbed his abs.

Ransom had to agree. The idea of stuffing his face with warm, melty cheese was nearly as appealing as the idea skipping dinner in favor of eating Rivet instead. Maybe sharing her with his partner if he was lucky. They hadn't ever had the opportunity to fuck a woman together, but he didn't think it would take any more convincing than it had to get Levi to agree to ordering dinner.

Probably less.

Damn it! Even hundreds of miles of open road hadn't

been enough to drive thoughts of the two of them, moments from caving to the undeniable chemistry they shared, out of his mind.

On the other hand, Rivet scooted away from them both, as if the suggestion of splitting a meal was more repulsive than the thought of sitting down to dinner with Angus himself. "You guys go ahead. I'm good."

"How can that be possible?" Ransom cut his stare back to her, scrutinizing her odd reaction. "We left early this morning. In the chaos and tension of everything that went down yesterday, I bet you didn't have anything more than I did, which was two puny bags of smashed chips from the police vending machine before they released us to Jordan's team."

Levi winced. He probably could tell that Ransom had been going nuts sitting in that tiny observation room. The institutionalized beige walls and glaring observation mirror had brought back far too many bad memories to facilitate proper digestion of even those bite-sized snacks he'd managed to choke down.

When they'd arrived on scene at the Middletown diner where he and Levi had accompanied Clive, the Wildfire sergeant-at-arms, they'd been able to keep the situation in hand and make sure Walker—Angus's son and Joy's lover—hadn't gotten his head blown off until the cops could take the guy into custody. He would be a key witness in their case. Especially if he also had first-hand knowledge of Rivet and Joy's mom's slaying.

Unfortunately, that had been hard to explain in a hurry. So the authorities had done their job and cuffed both Levi and him before they'd realized exactly who and what they were. The press of cold, hard steel on his wrists had nearly driven Ransom insane.

He wouldn't survive if they locked him up again. This time for good.

It would be better if he died bringing Wildfire to justice. Maybe then it would balance the scales for the wrongs he'd committed. He tried to be as good of a person as he was capable of every minute he still breathed to make up for the past. That included taking care of Levi. And now Rivet too.

So why didn't she want to eat?

She shrugged, putting his senses on high alert. "You're not saying you're not hungry. So why not eat? Are you nervous?"

He could understand that given the tangle his own guts had been in lately. Considering what they were up against and the increased dangers they would face as they tried to wrap up this case in a pretty, jail-orange bow, it was natural to be apprehensive. The odds were not in their favor.

"I'm not an idiot." She glared at him. "Of course I'm anxious, but that doesn't mean I'm going to back out or anything like that. I'm used to this, remember? Worry about yourself. Get your food."

Levi snorted. Probably because he knew Ransom.

There wasn't a chance he was going to let it go. Though he'd failed epically before, he had some kind of built-in protector instincts that he couldn't seem to shake. Even now.

"If it's not that, then why don't you want to share some grub with us?" Levi wasn't about to relent either. There was a reason he was Ransom's best—and only—friend. Of course his voice was low and charming, cajoling, a lot more persuasive than Ransom's typical growl.

"I can't eat a lot, okay?" Rivet hugged her middle. "I

have to stay slim so that I look like the immature man they expect me to be. If I'm not careful, I get curvy very quickly. As it is, these binders are about to suffocate me. I can't wait for the day I can throw them in the garbage."

"Hold up." Ransom stiffened, and not in a fun way. "You're telling me you're on some kind of starvation diet so you can be skinny enough for Wildfire?"

"I can't be bending over in the shop with a voluptuous ass or hips that don't look straight and lean. It's bad enough that my chest isn't flat even with these things on." Rivet waved her hands at her baggy T-shirt and the hoodie she'd left on over it even now.

He'd never quite realized that she swam in those layered, oversized clothes on purpose. It had made her seem scrawny and...exactly like she'd needed for them to believe she was a lanky dude who hadn't filled out yet.

He cursed.

"I hated this shit before. But now it's even less okay." Levi drew a deep shaky breath.

"You two concentrate on what you need to do to make your bosses happy and leave my parts of this scam to me." Rivet held her head at an angle, defiance rolling off her in waves. "What I'm doing works. Let's not change anything now."

Though he might have been the more rational of their duo, Levi wasn't a pushover. "My job is to make sure the three of us come out of this alive. That includes refusing to allow you to pass out tomorrow while doing critical shit —like riding the rest of the way to Wildfire and facing the gang or Angus after who knows how long going hungry. When's the last time you ate something?"

Rivet shrugged. "I honestly don't remember."

Ransom snatched a glossy card stained with greasy

fingerprints from the table. It held a variety of local takeout numbers. He twisted, nearly ripping the phone's receiver from its yellowed plastic cradle and held it out to Levi. Enough of this shit.

Though the corners of his eyes and mouth crinkled, none of that tension transferred to his partner's voice. He sounded calm and relaxed. Damn, he was good at this subterfuge shit. Much better than Ransom, whose emotions were starting to get the best of him. He was more of a smash-and-grab man than one who operated with any amount of finesse.

"Hi, I'd like to place an order for a large pepperoni pizza, some breadsticks, a six pack, and three bottles of water."

Ransom knew the situation was dire when the man got himself a couple of beers to make it through the night. He didn't usually drink while they were on the job. Or maybe he'd intended those for Ransom and Rivet. Either way, the three of them were going to eat, drink, and chill. Enjoy the last night they had of relative calm.

If they didn't, they might implode before they even arrived back in Wildfire territory.

The reality was they'd laid a lot of groundwork already. This was an endgame. They needed one more critical piece of irrefutable evidence that would nail Angus for good. Directly. They already had Clive, with all his damning implications. It was only a matter of time before the ex-sergeant-at-arms agreed to a deal, so long as the authorities kept him alive.

Angus was no idiot. He had to know it too. Ransom's hope was that he would do something to try to get Clive and they would be there to prove it. It wouldn't take long, which was for the best. None of them were going to last much longer, on edge, pushing their luck to the breaking point already. It was kind of a miracle that the three of them hadn't been busted yet.

He hoped they could go in, get what they needed, and be done. For good.

Rivet could live her best life at Hot Rides, with her sister and family, and a job she rocked.

But then what would happen to Levi? And him?

Rivet groaned when Levi hung up. "I hate you both."

"I'm not saying you have to eat the whole thing. A slice. A beer. That's all I'm asking." Ransom might have laid it on a little thick when he added, "We're in this together now. If something happens to you or is about to, do you really think Levi will hesitate to blow his cover? You have to think of the team."

Rivet rolled her eyes and gave him the finger so Levi came from a different angle. It was weird to see him play good cop for once. Usually they were bad thug and badder thug.

"While we're waiting, you should make yourself comfortable. Get out of those things, so you can at least breathe." Ransom figured Levi barely stopped himself from offering to undress her.

Good thing he had, though, because he knew as well as both Levi and Rivet did that they wouldn't stop there.

Her eyes were molten when they met Levi's, kick starting Ransom's jealousy once more.

Still, she didn't make any lewd suggestions Levi wouldn't be able to resist. Instead, she nodded, then slid her legs off the side of the bed. "Would you guys mind if I take a shower? I'd like to soak up the last of the hot water I'll probably see for a while."

"What do you mean?" Ransom asked.

"The apartment over the garage that I rent from Angus doesn't have any. Plus I'm always worried about staying naked for too long. Just in case someone decides to bust in on me. Or there's trouble and I can't wrap myself properly before I need to be downstairs." She didn't turn around as she headed for the bathroom, which was probably for the best.

Otherwise she might have been frightened by his expression, which he couldn't school nearly as well as Levi. This was too much. And yet he and Levi were escorting her right back into the thick of things.

If he hadn't already been going to hell, he would have figured he'd earned a one-way ticket for his involvement in this bullshit scheme. He swore then and there that Rivet wasn't going to be another casualty—totally innocent or not—of the Wildfire nation.

5

"**Y**ou had to get pepperoni, didn't you? Motherfucker." Rivet sniffed the air, then collapsed against the headboard. Her damp hair, slicked to her skull, lent her a chic androgynous look that Levi couldn't deny he found far more intoxicating than the beers he had ordered to try to set a more casual, comfortable tone between them.

One that would hopefully allow her to relax enough to at least eat a modest dinner and get a decent night's rest before they had to face Wildfire again.

Ransom laughed with his mouth half full of pizza. It wasn't often Levi heard the deep rumble, though he was interested to see that Rivet brought it out of his roommate far more often than Levi's own company ever had. "It's pretty damn good too. Way better than I expected for middle of fucking nowhere."

When Rivet leaned forward, practically drooling, Levi realized she was too hungry, too tempted to resist much longer. She was crumbling. Perfect.

So he made a show of scooping a couple more pieces

onto his plate and licking his fingers one by one. He closed his eyes halfway and hummed. He must have been a little too convincing because when he opened them both Ransom and Rivet were staring at him instead of the triangle of doughy deliciousness in his hand.

"What?" he mumbled around a full mouth.

Ransom turned to Rivet and said, "If it's him or the pizza, you should let yourself eat. At least that's a necessary evil and a whole lot less dangerous in the long run."

Rivet sighed, then nodded curtly. "Fine. You're right about that."

She hopped off the bed and plucked the smallest slice from the wedge of remaining pizza. Watching her eat in bed was probably the most erotic thing Levi had ever witnessed in his life. And that included Ransom's face when he'd finally caved to the desire between them and unloaded deep inside Levi for the first time.

That thought inspired him to chug half a beer. It did absolutely nothing to cool him off.

In fact, he choked when Rivet said, "Fuck it," cracked one open, then followed suit.

He did his best not to get drunk on the job but there were times, like when they hung out in the clubhouse collecting dirt, where it would have been obvious if he didn't partake at least some minimum amount. He'd seen Rivet do the same periodically, though she often used her duties at the garage as a reason to abstain.

He suspected she also did it because she was a bit of a lightweight. Literally and figuratively.

Given how many secrets she was hiding, being intoxicated could become fatal fast. So he took it as a compliment that she shared not only the pizza but the beer with him and Ransom.

She ate slowly, savoring every last morsel of the indulgence. Levi watched each bite that passed between her lips, and each swipe of her tongue over them after. When the three of them had demolished the pizza, and Levi was wondering if he could talk them into a second round, Rivet stood and stretched. "We should take shifts on watch. What order should we go in?"

Ransom folded his hands over his washboard abs, honed during the time he hadn't had much else to do but work out, and leaned back in his chair. "I'm good for a while. You two go ahead. Try to get some rest."

Levi's eyes widened. Him and Rivet? In the same bed? Hell no.

Then again, given the state of the motel carpet, he'd probably need a hazmat suit to endure a night down there. Maybe he could sleep in the tub or something.

"Jesus, Levi." Rivet snorted. "Don't look so scared. I don't bite. And I'll do my best not to jump you if you're not into it."

"I am." Why the hell had he said that? Except that it was true and he was losing his mind sharing this small space with her. Letting her strut into danger when he could have kept her safer by leaving her behind was doing strange things to him. He wanted to claim her. Protect her. And he couldn't do either. "I mean, I would be if we weren't in this situation."

"You're distracted," Ransom bitched again. "You have twelve hours max to get your head on straight before it's going to cost someone big time. Can you live with yourself if your dick gets one of us killed? Yourself included?"

"You know...that's a good point, Ransom. Maybe it

would be better for us to screw around tonight, while we can, and get whatever this is out of our systems." Rivet shrugged one shoulder as if she hadn't just given him an insta-boner.

His body said *hell yes*. His brain, on the other hand...

"No way," Levi insisted, yet he didn't back away.

Surprisingly Ransom didn't echo his objection. Instead he stared between Rivet and Levi, back and forth for several seconds, then—as if she was his own personal pizza—proclaimed, "Maybe Rivet's right."

"She is?" Levi must have been stunned since he slipped instead of saying *he* is. And that simply could never happen again once they left this room. Like a lot of other things. Including getting it on.

"I am." Rivet nodded. "I ate your pizza. Now it's your turn..."

Eat her? He would love to.

6

_____

Rivet couldn't believe she'd propositioned Levi. Aside from the fact that he was a law enforcement officer of some sort or other, he was worldly, experienced, and entirely out of her league. It must have been the damn beer on a mostly empty stomach. Okay, no, fine. It was his ass, and his eyes, and the core of goodness that she had always been able to sense within him despite the sinister outer trappings of his Wildfire cut.

When he'd talked to her, he'd always looked her in the eye. He'd never made her do grunt work or talked down to her simply because she was a peon in the club ranks.

And she wasn't going to lie, at least not to herself.

She needed someone to hold her and make her feel good in case this was the last time she had the chance to really live before everything went to shit.

Levi looked at Ransom, his head dipped, his entire body taut and coiled. He seemed torn, probably because this was his career as well as his personal life that they could be screwing up.

If he was counting on Ransom to dissuade him, as his partner had earlier, he would be disappointed. Something had shifted in Ransom. She'd practically seen it happening when he'd gone overprotective about her eating. Instead of chaperoning, trying to keep them apart, he was pushing them together, even if it was only for this brief moment in time.

He waved toward Rivet and the frumpy mattress. "Do what you gotta do. I'm going to keep an eye on the parking lot and make sure no one sneaks up on you while you're distracted."

"You mean you're going to stay while we...?" Rivet's eyes grew wide and she wondered what she'd gotten herself into. Could she really get it on with Levi while Ransom sat less than two feet away?

She thought for a moment of her sister and how Joy was clearly in love with both Walker and Dane. There was no way two sisters could get that lucky, could they?

"I would step outside, but..." Ransom hesitated.

Levi shook his head. "Not worth the risk. Stay here, where no one can see you. If Rivet is as bold as she's trying to pretend, she shouldn't care who sees us fuck. Isn't that right?"

His grin turned wolfish as he stared her down. Some of the gang mentality might have worn off on him, but she knew that if she told him she'd changed her mind, he would let her go. And that was the difference between civilized men and bandits.

If he thought for one second that intimidation would work on her, he hadn't been paying attention. She'd lived in the midst of her enemies for damn near two years now. And if she could take this one selfish thing for herself before she put her life on the line again, so be it.

Somehow the idea of Ransom listening in, practically watching them...well, it didn't make her any less horny, even if she didn't plan to admit it out loud.

"Absolutely." Rivet clutched the hem of her black T-shirt, wishing like hell it was the neon purple cold-shoulder crushed velvet dress she'd worn to her meeting with Walker, Dane, and Joy as Sevan. At least then she'd felt pretty. Now she was plain as she could make herself.

She thought of the scorching looks Levi had leveled at her, both in the clubhouse and outside the bathroom at the mountain home shared by Jordan, Kason, and Wren. Somehow, he liked both sides of her.

Which only made her crave him extra. She needed him more than she'd needed the slice of pizza he and Ransom had fed her, and she was going to enjoy his touch, the raw and honest contact, every bit as much.

She whipped the cotton over her head and dangled it from her fingers. Of course, standing there in front of him with her breasts exposed, the rouged indentations left by the binders crisscrossed her bare skin. It felt strange and scary to put herself on display after hiding at all costs for so long.

As if he knew, Levi reached for her, gathering her to his own broad chest and smothering her in a warm embrace. He rubbed the marks on her back before tipping his head forward and resting it against hers so he could stare directly into her eyes.

"I'm going to take care of you, I swear." He hugged her to him.

"I don't need you to." She didn't. Really. But that didn't mean she didn't want him to even if she hated that part of herself. The weak part. "How about you let *me* take care of *you* instead?"

"Whatever you want." He waited for direction.

It did something to her that he surrendered control. When in her life had she ever had that before? It was empowering and such a turn on she thought she might come simply from the anticipation of what was ahead.

Rivet grabbed Levi's shirt and shoved until he landed on his back, bouncing a bit on the squeaky springs before coming to rest. Then she climbed on top of him, her chest still on display. While raking his stare over her breasts, he seemed even hungrier than when he'd accepted the pizza from the delivery guy.

He lifted his hand to cup one in his palm. She shuddered. There was something about putting all her trust and faith in him—*them*—that simultaneously thrilled and terrified her. She glanced over at Ransom to find his jaw set, his profile harsh in the ugly orange light streaming in from the lamps outside. Was he going to peek? Or stay frozen like some sort of human gargoyle, protecting them while they released some of the pressure between them?

Making herself vulnerable in front of them both also made her feel as if she had some right to demand they put as much on the line as she was. She returned her focus to Levi and the massage he'd started on her breast. It felt incredible, smoothing out the ridges left by the fabric that had distorted her body.

"So...you're into men and women, is that it?" Rivet wondered aloud as he brushed the hardened tip of her nipple with the pad of his thumb. It certainly wasn't his first time playing with a boob. His expert-level caresses had her turned on faster than her bike could go zero to sixty.

"Yup." Levi showed her with his continued

explorations that he craved her just as much now as he had when he'd thought she was the young man she played so well. He probably didn't mean to, but he glanced over at Ransom, who didn't seem to give a shit that his partner was about to have his dick buried in someone else.

Of course, Rivet noticed the tiny wince that marred Levi's perfect lips. "Him?"

"Huh?" He played dumb and tried to distract her by sliding his hands to her shoulders and pulling her forward so he could use his tongue instead of his fingers. It was nearly enough to work. Actually, it did derail her line of questioning for a minute or two, while he licked and sucked and inspired her hips to start rocking so that she rode the impressive bulge in his jeans as he toyed with her.

But the lingering thought refused to fade completely. It was too seductive in its own right.

"Ransom," she sighed. The other man jerked as if she'd called out to him instead of referring to him. She speared her hands into Levi's golden hair and tugged until he had to look up at her. "You have sex with him?"

Levi shifted his icy blue gaze toward the other guy. As if he hadn't heard their not-so-private conversation, Ransom didn't deny it, so neither did Levi. "Sometimes."

As she opened her mouth to pry a little more, he added, "When we're desperate."

Ransom's breath whooshed out. Had that been news to him?

Had Levi hurt him with his proviso? Or had he simply been shocked that Levi didn't deny they fooled around? Something in her gut told her it was the former.

"I mean, Ransom's not really into guys, but he makes

do when I'm the only mouth or ass he has access to, you know? For me, it's just that it's a risk. One I don't take lightly. Otherwise I'd be begging for his cock all the time." Now it was Levi's turn. He winced, flashing that tiniest bit of insecurity, letting her glimpse a wound deep within him.

Who'd made him feel that he was less of a man because of who he was attracted to? She added whoever it was to her hate list.

Wow, she'd finally met two other people as completely fucked up as she was. It made her like Levi and Rasom even more. And want to fix them, like no one had ever done for her.

While she couldn't work miracles in an evening, she at least knew one way to ease Levi's suffering. "Well, I've wanted you for months even though there were plenty of other dicks around to pick from. Not that I would have..."

"It wouldn't have ended well." Levi's grip on her shoulders increased. "You know you can't do that, right?"

Rivet's spine went ramrod stiff. "Just because I'm about to fool around with you doesn't mean I spread my legs or blow any dude in the clubhouse. And if you remember, it was *you* that kissed *me*."

"I know. I'm sorry. I shouldn't have." Levi groaned. "And here I am about to do it again and again until we're in danger of passing out from lack of oxygen."

"You are?" Rivet softened, her ire melting in the face of his honest desire.

"If you'll still let me." He didn't force her closer or flip them over, instead letting her decide.

"He didn't mean any harm," Ransom said quietly, proving that he was every bit as engaged in their conversation as the two of them were. Whether he was talking about Levi's possessiveness about who she fucked or the comment he'd made about sleeping with Ransom out of desperation, maybe both, she wasn't sure.

But if he was willing to give the guy a pass, so was she.

Rivet nodded slowly, biting her lip, imagining what it would feel like—very soon—when Levi's mouth was planted there instead of her own teeth. Before finding out for certain, she gathered the hem of his shirt in her hands and began to walk it up his torso, revealing a physique that had more in common with action figures than with the body of any guy she'd had the opportunity to touch in real life before.

"Damn, you're beautiful," she murmured to him as the full extent of his buffness was put on display. For her. It might not be traditional to think of a guy that way, but that didn't make it any less true.

"Same goes." He smiled as he shrugged out of the light cotton and left it crumpled on the pillow beside his head. The fact that he thought so when she didn't look like any movie star she'd ever seen made a lump form in her throat.

What they were doing might be—no, definitely was—foolish, but she didn't give a shit. She deserved this single self-indulgence after so long happiness starved.

From his post, Ransom huffed at their exchange. He muttered something under his breath that sounded like, "Damn straight. Both are."

When she glanced over her shoulder to try to read his expression, Levi reached for her and drew her close to him once more. The heat of his skin pressed to hers as they collided chest to chest made her breath catch. He nuzzled her neck, causing her eyes to roll back in her head before whispering, "Don't worry, he's paying attention. Maybe if we put on a good enough show, he'll cave."

She liked the way he thought.

And the way he kneaded her back, encouraging her to arch against him and unite them completely from waists to shoulders.

It felt so damn good to be fused with someone—anyone, really, but especially him—again.

Rivet skimmed her hands from his shoulders around his back, mimicking the sensual massage he was giving her. Then she lifted her head and sought his mouth with hers. When their lips locked there was no attempt to be subtle on either of their parts.

They came together to unleash the pent-up passion from their taboo longing.

Fuck it. So what if doing this sooner might have gotten her killed? It might have been worth it, so long as Angus was dealt with first.

No. She refused to think of that bastard now.

When Levi reclined fully, she followed him down, straddling his hips while still devouring him. His hands gripped her ass and directed her to grind her mound along the length of his denim-covered cock. Even through his clothes, she could tell it was going to be as impressive as the rest of him.

It was too dangerous to have toys hanging around her apartment above Angus's garage. She was looking forward to being filled as she hadn't been since she'd broken up with her last boyfriend about two years ago, pre-Wildfire. Maybe it was because of their situation and the adrenaline high she'd been riding nearly every day she spent embedded in the motorcycle club, but she didn't remember ever getting this turned on by Chris during their entire relationship.

Then again, Levi was a man—all grown, all over—whereas Chris had been a dude more along the lines of what everyone thought Rivet to be. Inexperienced, immature, and eager though not very skilled.

Levi had an inherent harshness to him that attracted Rivet and made her want to smooth a few of his sharp edges. They made out until, true to his word, sparkles danced in her vision.

So she broke them apart and scooted down until she sat just above his knees.

That left his waistband free and clear for her to grab. Something made her hesitate.

She looked down into his clear, bright eyes and waited for him to give her a definitive green light. She didn't have to wait long. He took her hands in his and placed them over the buckle of his belt. "Anything you want is fine. There's nothing you could do to me that I haven't dreamt about doing with you already."

She raised a brow. Could he really mean that?

Because she thought she was the only one who'd been obsessed.

And now that she knew what was between him and Ransom, her fantasies were rapidly expanding to include him as well.

"Just me or me and him?" She jerked her head toward Ransom.

"Will it freak you out if I say both?" he wondered, surprisingly open after keeping himself shielded in her presence for so long. She realized then that although she'd had some inkling as to the man he was, she hadn't truly known the depths he was capable of taking her to. Until now.

And now she wanted to find out everything about him.

Especially the places he liked to be touched, and how to drive him wild with pleasure.

"Nope. It's kind of hot. I never really considered that sort of thing until I saw how fucking happy Joy is with Walker and Dane. Or Jordan with Wren and Kason. I had no idea how much fun I was missing out on." Rivet had let some of the best years of her life go by, her own goals and needs unfulfilled in exchange for seeking justice for her mother.

It had been worth it.

But that didn't mean that she didn't regret the need for it at all. If only she'd been wiser, she might not have made such a tragic mistake. Her mom would still be here. She would be managing her grandfather's shop like he'd intended instead of having sold it off to strangers.

And...well...

She also wouldn't be there with Levi right then. So at least one positive had come out of the disaster. Rivet planned to make the most of the one perk she had.

"No need to miss out tonight." Levi lifted his ass from the bed, jutting his hips and the distinct bulge in his pants up at her. "Go ahead. Take what you need."

Rivet nodded, then slipped black leather through the silver metal holding it. The belt was thick and heavy in her grasp, reminding her of Levi himself. She brushed the ends aside and unbuttoned his jeans before sliding his zipper down.

It surprised her, though she couldn't say why, to see that he wasn't wearing any underwear. His cock was right there, ready and very eager for her to touch and lick and fuck.

"Damn," she murmured when she pushed aside the edges of his pants and revealed him fully.

Ransom snorted at that.

"Hey, just because I don't have some kind of monster cock like you doesn't mean I don't have enough to get the job done!" Levi glared at his best friend.

Rivet whipped her stare to the other man. If he was bigger than Levi, she was going to have to find a way to check that out for herself. Someday. But what if this was the only day?

With one hand she fisted Levi and ran her fingers along his shaft, measuring him with her languid strokes. He hissed, his cock jerking in her grip.

"I've got no complaints."

"Only because you haven't seen what he's packing." Levi gritted his teeth and braced himself as if it took every ounce of his energy to stay still and let her explore. Hell, maybe it did.

"I don't believe that." She shot a coy smile in Ransom's direction. "But if he wants to try to prove me wrong, I'm not going to complain."

He didn't take the bait. Instead he gripped the edge of the table as if it would keep him anchored and concentrated extra hard on the nothing outside the window.

"Sorry." Levi grimaced.

Rivet shrugged. "I'm not sad about having you to play with, Levi. I've spent a lot of time thinking about this too, you know."

"Then let's get to it before something interrupts us and I die of blue balls."

7

Levi shoved his pants down and lifted his ass. So Rivet helped strip them off him before sinking between his legs. She caressed his sac with the tips of her fingers, watching it draw up close to his body.

"They don't look blue to me." She grinned up at him a moment before licking a line along the underside of his shaft. She wondered how much she could tease him before he cracked. Before the guy she knew he was broke free of his false reserve and wrested control from her.

She wouldn't mind.

In fact, she was looking forward to it.

She wanted to let go. To have someone else be in charge for once. To enjoy and not have to think or plan or consider every angle. Rivet needed to be swept away by someone strong and capable so she could let go of her worries and simply enjoy.

So she baited Levi.

Rivet took hold of his cock and aimed it at her parted lips. She stared straight into his eyes as she fed it to herself. So she saw the instant his mind shut down and his instincts kicked in.

"Fuck, yes." He coached her. "Suck it. Just a little. Get me good and wet. Totally hard. So I can fuck you as best as I can."

Didn't have to tell her twice. She did as he commanded, because she craved the same thing. He made a mouthful, that was for sure, but she tried her best to relax enough that he could slip almost completely inside, even if that meant taking part of him into her throat.

It had been a while since she'd attempted those advanced maneuvers, and never on anyone as well-endowed as him. Which was probably obvious when she started to choke. Levi was there in an instant, his hands on her shoulders, inching her back and holding her while she cleared her airway and lunged forward for more.

"Probably best if you don't." He groaned. "You're a little too good at that."

She would have argued except selfishly she hoped their ride wouldn't be a quick spin around the block. Apparently he was on the same page because he used the pressure on her shoulders to nudge her, twisting her until she lost her balance and tumbled to the bed beside him.

"My turn," he said with a wolfish smile that made a mockery of his seeming surrender.

"Have at it." Rivet wasn't about to stop him.

Before she could do it herself, he'd unfastened her pants and dragged them and her padded boxer briefs down her legs. He traced the slight curve of her hips, apparent without the camouflage of ill-fitted clothing. Still, she wasn't womanly like her sister.

He placed a kiss on each of her hipbones, muttering

something about eating all the damn pizza she wanted soon.

But if she couldn't have more dinner, she'd gladly take Levi for dessert instead.

Rivet couldn't help the moan that floated from her parted lips when he pressed on the insides of her knees, urging her to make room for him between them. When she did, he mirrored her earlier position. Where she had been teasing at first, he wasn't.

Levi buried his face in her pussy as if he was as ravenous as she had been when he'd waved that pepperoni beneath her nose. He bombarded her senses with swipes of his tongue, suction from his lips, and the press and release of his hands on her hips.

And that was before he groaned against her, adding vibration to the mix.

Rivet seized up, a spike of pleasure drawing her tight, her back arching in response. It was thrilling, and risky, and so damn good she could hardly stand it.

When she gasped, Ransom shifted as if it was getting more and more difficult for him to remain blasé. Her attention didn't stay on him for long. Because Levi turned out to be even better at eating her out than he was at pretending to be a badass biker.

He really got into it, like it gave him every bit as much pleasure as it did her when he tasted the slickness he was inspiring between her legs. He licked, sucked, and even nibbled on her, paying rapt attention to her reactions, then doing more of the things that made her sigh, moan, and gasp.

Levi didn't do anything half-assed, and this was no exception.

It didn't take long before her toes were curled and her

pelvis strained toward him, pressing her pussy tight to his face. Her hand snaked down and gripped his head, terrified that he would stop and leave her riding this white-hot edge of rapture.

She shouldn't have worried.

He looked up at her, amusement and appreciation dancing in his eyes. It was almost like he was daring her to come. Her body reacted without input from her rational mind. She unraveled, shocking herself with the intensity of her orgasm.

Levi knew how to play her, or maybe they simply got off on the same things.

Either way, she threw back her head, arched, then shuddered. Her breasts felt heavy and full, so she cupped them. Squeezing them only increased the sensations rioting through her nerve endings, making her shout his name while her entire body clenched and released.

A profound sense of relief washed over her along with her rapture. It felt amazing to let herself go and rely on someone else, even if it was reckless and stupid.

The endorphin rush that followed made her high on ecstasy.

That must have been why she yearned for more after one of the most epic climaxes of her life.

Rivet reached down to where Levi was nuzzling her, lapping at the proof of her pleasure and helping her come back to reality. Except that wasn't what she wanted at all. She would do whatever it took to stay here in this bubble with him for as long as possible.

Besides, she had a feeling that while this was already the best sexual experience of her life, it was about to get a whole lot better.

She hooked her hands beneath his arms and yanked,

encouraging him to slide upward. He reached beside her to grab his T-shirt and used it to wipe his face. The motion did nothing to erase the grin there, though.

Rivet couldn't recall ever seeing him smile like that. He was even more handsome, the typical seriousness he embodied muted. It was only then that she realized he was just as broken inside as her. Maybe someday she would find out why.

If sex with him made for a temporary cure for them both, she wasn't about to deny it to either of them.

"Good?" he asked.

"It was. The best. Thank you." She was still struggling to catch her breath.

"You're welcome." He kissed her with a tenderness she hadn't expected. That sent another wave of tremors through her. But he must have misunderstood, because he started to roll to his side as if he was about to take care of himself.

Hell no.

"Levi, we're not done here." She kept him from going too far by propping one foot flat on the bed and using her knee as a guardrail.

"We're not?" he asked. When had anyone cared so much about her needs that they'd been willing to put them above their own? His steely cock made it obvious he was dying to fuck. And yet, he'd walk away if she told him to.

"I need more." She reached down and stroked his hard-on. Like she would let the chance to be joined with him—or honestly most any other human being—slip by? No way.

"Thank god." He swiped her hand away and crawled up her body, covering her with his much larger one as he aligned their torsos. He took her hands in his, palm to palm, fingers interlocked, and held them against the pillow on either side of her head.

For a few moments, he simply stared down at her, scanning her face and staring into her eyes. She wondered if he appreciated what he saw or if, like her, he was ravenous for companionship and closeness. Maybe it was some of both, because when he kissed her again, she sensed something different.

Something more personal than had been there before.

Or maybe it was her imagination, which was going wild, speculating about what the very near future was going to be like.

As they made out, Levi shifted over her. He rocked, sliding his cock along her slit, the blunt heat rubbing her clit and making her twitch. Though she'd come hard minutes earlier, it seemed like that orgasm had only primed her body for more pleasure.

So she adjusted her legs, splaying them wider to allow Levi more room to work between them.

They were so caught up in the moment, she didn't even object when the tip of his cock began to nudge her opening, pressing a tiny bit inside. Still bare.

Ransom took his post looking out for them seriously, though. He cleared his throat loudly.

When Levi froze, then shifted his gaze to Ransom, Rivet did the same. For the first time she was irritated with his presence. She needed Levi to push forward, fill her, and wipe away the fear and doubt and anger that had occupied her mind for so long.

The other guy tipped to one side as he fished in his pocket for his wallet. "Better use this. Never say I didn't have your back."

He tossed a condom to Levi, who caught it without separating them. Levi ripped the packet open with his teeth, then shifted until he sat on his heels.

Watching him roll the latex down his hard-on both thrilled her—to imagine it would soon be buried within her, making her scream his name—and disappointed her.

Would it have been so terrible to have fucked with nothing between them? So that she didn't have to be separated from him by even that thin barrier? Well, only if they lived to face the consequences, she supposed. And the deeper they got, the less likely she thought that was.

Thinking of her sister, her niece—goddaughter—and how happy the baby had made Walker, Dane, and Joy, Rivet wondered if getting pregnant would really have been so bad. Of course, that would make it really hard to pretend she was the dude Wildfire thought she was.

Shoving the thought away to study at another time, when she wasn't about to explode from anticipation and rapture, she reached for Levi's erection and aimed it where she wanted it most.

He rumbled her name, low and harsh, before tipping forward, blanketing her with his body. She felt safe. Protected. And desired.

Everything she'd been missing these past two years. Hell, maybe forever. Her grandparents had done what they could to fill the void left by her mother, promised Rivet that it was Angus's fault she'd left and couldn't come back. But the deeper she'd burrowed into Wildfire, the more she realized that might not exactly have been true.

If her own mother could leave her, what did that mean for anyone else?

Fortunately, this was only about right then. That moment. One night.

That's all that counted. And in that instant, Levi gave her everything she needed.

"You ready?" he asked her, as if he could sense the turn of her thoughts.

Rivet needed him to distract her from them before they stole her enjoyment. "Been waiting forever. Come on."

He grinned. "I like it when you're pushy."

"Good. Because I'm going to get downright nasty if you don't fuck me. Right now." She hooked a leg around his hip, the arm from the opposite side of her body across his back, and tugged until he was plastered against her again.

The weight and heat of him was like the world's best security blanket. A sexy one, of course.

He didn't waste any time recapturing her mouth and kissing her as he crawled along her body, arranging them to suit him best. This time, when his cock began to prod at her core, neither of them stopped. Fortunately, Ransom didn't have any further objections either.

Levi pressed into her, not getting very far at first. The initial penetration rocked her, making her heart stop in her chest then beat twice as hard. Part of her resisted, her defenses ingrained, until she reminded herself that this was what she coveted. To let him in. To join together to both of their advantages.

His kisses turned seductive instead of demanding. He was trying to calm her down, get her to relax so he could embed himself within her. And it was working. The pressure of his blunt head against her folds eased as he began to sink into her inch by inch.

After each bit of progress, he backed out then began again, coating his shaft in her arousal and easing the way forward for them both.

The sensations caused by his invasion blanked her mind, giving her blessed relief from her apprehensions, her fears, and her insecurities. It was the most incredible thing she'd ever felt, shockingly good and only a tiny bit uncomfortable despite how he stretched her to fit.

"Am I hurting you?" he whispered against her lips.

"Not much. Keep going." She answered honestly, touched that he even gave a shit. Yeah, he was nothing like the rest of the Wildfire gang or even the guys she'd dated before.

Levi slowed down, using one hand to pet her from her shoulder to her elbow and back as he turned leisurely in his approach. He coaxed her body into accepting him and welcoming him as if she had a lot more practice at it than she really did.

"Damn, you're tight. So petite." He groaned. "Tell me if I'm too much."

"Haven't you noticed I like rough rides?" She grinned up at him, because it was true. She had to be sure he respected her enough to let loose. That he wouldn't hold anything back from her.

Rivet could handle this. She could handle him.

8

Levi's hand wandered back up to Rivet's collarbone then down to her breast. He gripped her harder this time, making her pussy flex around him. They both cried out as she massaged his dick involuntarily.

And when he finally reversed his motion and began to back out, her body did everything in its power to cling to him, enhancing the impact of his motions. The return thrust was smoother and even more satisfying. After a few more repetitions, in and out, he began to piston into her faster, making both of their breathing grow ragged.

The bed squeaked and the headboard tapped the wall in a distinct pattern no one on the other side of the wall would mistake for anything but exactly what they were doing.

At least he was right there with her, equally as dazzled by the way their bodies fit together and influenced each other. For several minutes, all she could do was cling to him and relish the wonder that they generated with the friction of their flesh against each other's.

One of his plunges hit some wondrous spot within her that made her call out his name.

"Yeah." He talked dirty to her, which did nothing to help her stay calm and collected. "Feel what I can do to you. Feel my dick inside you, stretching you, filling you, and unraveling you stroke by stroke."

Ransom cursed in the background, as if he too was impacted by Levi's string of sexy filth.

"What's he doing?" Levi asked softly in her ear without pausing his motion to see for himself.

Rivet turned her head and took in Ransom's locked legs and balled fists, which were probably the only thing keeping him from at least taking his own cock into his hand and joining them remotely in slaking his desire. His shoulders rose and fell more sharply than they had before. He definitely wasn't unaffected by Levi and Rivet's performance.

"He's getting off on listening to you fuck me. Maybe on watching some too, in the reflection on the window." Rivet sighed as she quivered around Levi. "Is it because he's imagining being me?"

She wouldn't blame him if he was jealous of her right then.

"Doubtful." Levi nipped her lower lip. "More like he's never seen me fuck before since usually it's him doing this to me."

She hugged Levi then as he kept up his pace within her. Had he needed this as desperately as she had? Had he gone too long without? Always giving it up to Ransom and never taking his share? Somehow she guessed it might even be some sort of self-inflicted penance to him. But for what?

She vowed to chase the demons from his gaze and leave only rapture behind.

Rivet squeezed him tighter with her legs, keeping him closer as she undulated beneath him to meet him stroke for stroke. "I'm glad I'm getting to see it. Feel it."

She moaned. Oh yeah, did she ever feel it.

The next few plunges of his cock within her were less steady, somewhat wild and unrestrained. What would he be like if Ransom joined them on the bed? Would Levi defer to the other man, letting his alpha flair melt away so that he could be like her, selfish and mindless with bliss while Ransom led them both in the pursuit of pleasure?

Would Levi enjoy being sandwiched between them, taking from Ransom while giving to her?

The thought alone caused a spasm that wrung his cock.

"You like the thought of him and me getting it on?" Levi asked as if he couldn't really believe it, another hint of that vulnerable place inside him peeking out. Still he drilled into her, harder and faster as she imagined what that would look like and Levi remembered it.

Rivet nodded, then clung to him. She regretted her short nails didn't allow her to mark his back and stake a claim. Levi was incredible. More than enough for her, but this side of him made her want him even more. Made her intent on showing him just how attractive she found his openness. "Probably about as much as you do."

"Yeah. Thinking of him makes me even harder." Levi didn't seem to mind that she was fantasizing about his friend while they fucked. In fact, it seemed to spur him on.

Unable to ignore their goading, Ransom got to his feet, bent in half with his hands braced on his knees for a few deep breaths. Was he going to give up his shitty attempt at indifference and join them in bed? Rivet wouldn't have objected if he had.

Instead, he paced to the door where he could see out the other side of the window. They all knew he wasn't really watching for Wildfire members. The lights of their bikes would shine right in the window and the rumble of their motors would likely rattle the door off its shoddy hinges.

Still, he didn't turn to face them, and certainly didn't attempt to come closer.

Rivet knew it made her greedy to be enjoying his partner's skills in bed so damn much and yet hope for more, but if she was going to have one last hoorah, she might as well go big.

"Are you really going to let your best friend suffer like that?" she asked Levi between parries of their tongues. "You know he wants this too even if he is too stubborn to do anything about it."

"Are you offering to take care of him? Or to let me do it while you're taking care of me?" Levi wondered, his mind clearly addled by passion. "Either way, I'm in. *So* in."

"I'm not." Ransom shook his head while keeping his back to them. "One of us has to stay alert."

Levi dropped his head and scrunched his eyes closed as if Ransom's rejection stung. Maybe he really believed his partner was only into him because he had no other options. Hell, for that matter, it could be true, though Rivet didn't think so. No, there was something more going on here. A gap she suddenly wanted to bridge between them.

"It won't hurt you to take a look, Ransom. Just a quick peek." Rivet's mischievous side came out to play. The clench of Levi's hands on her hips and the way his next stroke was twice as sharp made her sure he didn't mind one bit.

When Ransom still didn't budge, she teased, "Are you afraid you're not going to be able to stay away if you do?"

"Maybe." He did glance over his shoulder then. His dark eyes went wide and he rotated, leaning his back against the door as if to ground himself. "Fuck, that's hot."

Rivet ran her hands down Levi's back and grabbed his ass, which clenched as he redoubled his efforts, pounding into her with small grunts that sent shockwaves through her entire body.

And though she was right there, teetering on the brink of another orgasm, she didn't tip over. Maybe because she was waiting for someone to tell her it was okay to fly. Or maybe because she didn't want what they were doing to end. Ever.

"Son of a bitch. The two of you are so fucking sexy." Ransom growled from his post near the door. "And together...you're lucky that bed hasn't caught on fire yet."

When Rivet looked up, she realized he had given up all pretense of indifference and was studying their actions. His feet were spread and he leaned back, his shoulders resting on the door. The bulge of his erection was obvious and impressive in his pants.

"You see what you do to him?" Levi asked her, pinning her with his much larger body. He ground against her, showing her that he obviously did and enjoyed the sight.

Rivet didn't bother to deny it when her pussy was practically smothering his cock. She nodded.

"Say it. So he can hear you," Levi commanded.

What the fuck kind of naughty rabbit hole had she fallen down? She'd never expected to find this on her path to destroying Angus, but she was glad for the detour. If she died, at least she knew she'd really lived for this one night first.

"I'm getting off on knowing he's turned on by what we're doing." She refused to look away from Levi's entrancing stare. She wasn't afraid of him or the desire they shared. How could she be when he was right there with her, his breathing ragged and sweat beginning to dot his temples?

"And what exactly are we doing?" Levi smiled softly at her as he caressed the insides of her wrists with his thumbs, making her shudder around him.

"We're fucking," Rivet murmured.

"Yes. We are. Finally." He ground into her so that they were joined completely. "And you're even more amazing than I ever imagined. Tight and slick and so fucking delicious I could eat you all night."

Ransom groaned at that.

"He loves oral." Levi's cock jerked within her. Apparently he liked it too, or maybe he liked the idea of Ransom going down on one or both of them.

She shuddered.

"You too, huh?" He laughed as he fucked her, an intoxicating blend of emotions she'd never indulged in before. "Sounds like we're a good match. The three of us."

The back of Ransom's head thunked against the door, threatening to put a dent in the flimsy panel. "You bastard. You know I have no willpower. No self-control."

Levi was obviously Ransom's pepperoni.

"Then get over here and take what you need." Levi teased, "She's so warm, and fucking incredible. You know you want to."

Ransom groaned. "It's been so long since I've fucked a woman. I almost forgot how soft a pussy is compared to..."

"Me." Levi did stutter then, his strokes becoming slightly uneven as he processed Ransom's seeming disappointment.

Rivet couldn't stand it anymore. The distance between the men and how badly they wished they could share this —her—with each other, even if they didn't know how to ask for what they craved.

So she did it for them.

"Ransom," she begged. "Please come over here. If we're in this together...the three of us...let's really be in it together."

He shook his head again, making Levi's cock wilt slightly.

Desperate times called for desperate measures, so she used the ammunition Levi had given her with his revelation about Ransom's weakness.

"I want to suck your cock, and feel safe between you for one fucking minute." Rivet gasped when Levi pulsed within her, clutching her to him as if he could give her everything she'd ever desired. "Give me...*us*...this. Please."

Things turned serious when Ransom approached warily, his hand tucked in his pants as if he couldn't wait another second for even that bit of relief. "Seeing you two like this... Damn. I've never been so hard in my life."

"Let us see," Levi demanded. "Unless you're a better man than me and can walk away right now."

Ransom snarled. "I'm not trying to hold out so I can look down at you two or some shit."

He marched to the side of the bed as if to prove it. "Fine. This whole fucking thing is one bad decision after another. Why not add another to the pile?"

Before Rivet or Levi could do it for him, Ransom ripped open his fly, allowing his cock to spring free. He roared as if the pressure of keeping his erection bound had been driving him insane.

Rivet could understand. She writhed so that her breasts rubbed against Levi's chest.

It felt so good to free herself from the confines the situation had trapped her in for years.

To be herself for one fucking night.

She reached out and grabbed Ransom's dick before he could back away again. She used the grip, her fingers barely touching around his girthy cock, to tug him nearer. His knees pressed against the edge of the mattress and she turned her head, inviting him into her open mouth.

"I know I shouldn't." He looked to Levi, who was working his own cock within her faster and faster with every minute that passed. "But I can't help myself."

"Do it," Levi told Ransom, reaching a hand out to rest on his friend's ass and shove him toward her. "You deserve this."

"Do I?" Ransom asked.

No one answered. Rivet couldn't because suddenly her mouth was full of him. And Levi didn't seem able because he was fascinated by the sight of Rivet blowing Ransom while he fucked her so damn well she was going to have to retire from sex after they finished that night. Nothing would ever live up to that moment. She'd peaked at twenty-two. This was it.

The best she could do was curl one hand around the back of Ransom's thigh to hold him close and make sure he didn't bail. She didn't know him well enough to say what he merited, but she suspected she wouldn't have been so damn attracted to him if he was the horrible person he seemed to consider himself to be.

Sometime when she had more than two functioning brain cells, she would think more about that.

"Well, at least you only asked him for a single minute." Levi grunted. "Because I'm not sure how much longer I'm going to last. Especially not while I'm watching you take us both. Damn, Rivet."

She chuckled at that, her body vibrating around him, making both of them moan. The audible response must have added to the effectiveness of her mouth and tongue on Ransom. He groaned.

How could this be so fun and so intense at the same time? Fucking them was giving her a high like she'd never experienced before. Maybe she was becoming addicted to adrenaline and poor decisions. Maybe she was more like her mother than she'd realized.

That sobering thought might have pulled her from her euphoria if it hadn't been for Levi. He surprised her when he kissed her and Ransom's cock where it protruded from her mouth. If Levi had been a lot for her, Ransom was impossible to swallow.

Levi murmured to her, "Let me help."

She released Ransom's cock with a wet pop that made him curse. Levi was there to take up where she'd left off. He angled his head and told Ransom, "Fuck my face."

"Shit, yes." The other man didn't even bother trying to resist anymore. Not when he so obviously needed the same things they did. "Look at you fucking that pussy. I bet it feels amazing on your dick. You're getting it good, aren't you?"

"Want a turn?" Rivet asked him, shocked that she could be so bold.

Levi hummed as if he approved. When he pulled off Ransom's dick, giving her another chance to take a few sucks and sample the pearly fluid at the tip, he added, "You do, don't you, Ransom? It would give me a break. Otherwise, I'm about to shoot. I don't want this to be done. Come on, help me out."

Ransom winced. "I only had one condom."

"Fuck." Levi snarled. "Then let's make the most of it."

Rivet felt guilty for the disappointment that washed over her. Especially because she didn't expect there to be another opportunity to make up for their lack of preparation.

Still, there was nothing wrong with what they were doing right then. It was by far the best sex she'd ever had. And she was going to fall with Levi. Any second.

He guaranteed it when he lifted up onto straight-locked arms, putting a tiny wedge of space between them, and told Ransom, "Rub her clit. Make her come so I can too. I'm going to blow you so well you can't help but come with us."

"I don't doubt that." Ransom ran his hand over Levi's head as if he was stroking a favorite pet. Hell, he probably was.

Levi moaned, then leaned down, taking Ransom's cock deep into his mouth in a single swoop.

He was talented, that was for sure. He was grace in motion as he kept pumping into her while sucking Ransom. Rivet had seen porn stars who were far less impressive than the man spreading her legs. She arched, quivering, and that was before Ransom's hand snaked between them.

His palm landed low on her belly with his fingers draped over her mound. And when his middle finger found her clit as if he had some sort of magnetic connection, she shouted out his name.

He rubbed circles around it in time to the plunging of Levi's cock within her, making sure that she was going to wring the most pleasure from her orgasm possible.

Levi groaned along Ransom's shaft.

"I bet she's getting even tighter on you. Hugging your cock as hard as your ass does to mine. Isn't she, Levi?" Whoa. This side of Ransom was one she hadn't ever seen before and one she never wanted to forget.

No wonder Levi let him take the lead in their bedroom.

She would too. In fact, she did.

Rivet looked up at him and he smiled, slow and wide. He knew he had them both.

"Yeah, and his cock feels so good in you, doesn't it? You're so fucking wet. I can't wait to taste you for myself." As if to prove it, he withdrew his hand, making her cry out. But he only left long enough to lick her juices from his digits before replacing them. "You're sweet, Rivet. Despite what you pretend."

"Fuck you." She groaned, making Levi laugh around Ransom's cock.

Ransom cursed as Levi's amusement played along his sensitive flesh. "Levi's taking care of that, isn't he? He's doing such a great job. I can't believe he's never tried to fuck me before."

Levi froze at that, then redoubled his pace. Did he want to make love to Ransom instead?

Rivet would have offered to let him, but she needed just a few more seconds for herself first.

And she hoped that Levi would come with her, not

leave her to experience such a devastating release all by herself. She shouldn't have worried.

Ransom's finger began to manipulate her clit again, this time flicking over it more directly once he tested the motion to make sure it wasn't too intense for her. He was an expert. A master at plying her body. So she let both him and Levi work.

Rivet closed her eyes, concentrating on the arousal spiraling higher and higher within her until it was impossible to deny any longer.

Her eyes flew open, she gasped, and her entire body drew tight.

"That's right, Rivet." Ransom growled at her. "Come. Come so hard you take Levi with you. If he does a good job, I'll feed him my come too."

Levi went wild. His thrusts turned into a frenzy of motion that lit up every nerve ending inside her. The ridge of his head tugged at the ring of muscles at her entrance on every backstroke, when he nearly—but not quite—slipped free of her.

And when he bottomed out, connecting them completely, she exploded.

Rivet clawed at his back with one hand while her other gripped Ransom's leg. The wail that escaped her was unrecognizable, a sound that had been caged within her with no outlet for years. She fell apart around Levi, her entire being dissolving and reforming as she came and came and came.

Within her, she felt him stiffen then buck, pumping his own seed into the condom Ransom had given him, filling it with jet after jet of his release.

"Yes. That's right. You're both so sexy. So perfect." Ransom groaned.

Despite his own climax, Levi didn't let go of his partner. Instead he sucked harder, his cheeks hollowing with the effort. Rivet aided him by switching her grip to cup Ransom's balls. The instant she brushed his tight sac, he roared.

Ransom grabbed Levi's head and fucked, plowing into his friend's mouth while his balls pulsed in her palm. He fed Levi every drop of his come, proof that he wasn't unaffected by their joining.

He came so hard and fast that a trickle of his semen escaped Levi's lips.

And as Rivet peaked and began to slide down the far side of her own climax, Levi kept rocking into her gently as he suckled Ransom's softening shaft.

Rivet could hardly breathe, but not because of Levi's body lying on her. It was the weight of what they'd done —and what the two men had shared with her, exposing their own secrets—that shook her to her soul.

No matter what she tried to tell herself, this had been so much more than a quickie. More than slaking a simple human desire. No, this had been...life-changing.

And maybe not only for her.

The three of them were bonded. A team. And they were going to need to stick together if they had any chance of surviving the next part of their journey. Who knew what might happen after that?

9

_____

Levi had never been so satisfied in his entire life. Still, he figured it might be possible to be even more contented. Unfortunately he couldn't say for sure, because Ransom hadn't given in and fucked him like they'd both obviously wished for, but he'd settle for what they had done, sharing Rivet and the moment. He hadn't realized quite how much he'd come to rely on his bond with Ransom until he'd faced going without it.

Even when he had another smoking hot partner to play with.

What did that mean for them when they finished this case? And what did it mean now that Rivet was in the picture? It complicated matters that were already touchy as fuck.

Rivet yawned, burrowed under the comforter and said, "Damn, I needed that."

Her similar bone-deep peacefulness touched Levi somewhere other than in his hormones. *Uh oh.*

He rubbed his chest and rolled toward her so he could study her serene, sleepy expression. Damn, she was even more beautiful when she was relaxed. The hard edge he'd come to associate with her had dissipated, leaving gentle curves and a hint of softness in its wake. Her eyes were clear and bright as they looked up at him.

"How the hell did you decide to do this for a living?" She didn't blink as she waited for his response. "You could have picked...well, anything. Why *this*?"

With his guard down, her question hit him right in the gut and twisted. How honest should he be? Levi balked when he considered her reaction, never mind Ransom's.

So he spit out the standard response he had to that question like it was some kind of reflex. "Same as you, really. I don't like seeing bad things happen to innocent people because of the actions of monsters like Angus."

Although that was the truth, he couldn't keep the bitterness from his tone when he conveyed it to her. He must be more exhausted than he thought, or fucking her had done something to him. Changed him. Maybe forever. He'd spent too much time in the cesspools of humanity.

After this, he might need to consider retiring, or at least taking some kind of mental health break to get himself together again.

"Nah, I don't think that's all of it." Rivet reached out and touched his cheek, drawing his stare back to hers. "This isn't a job. Don't give me that shit. It's more than that. Who got hurt because of Angus?"

"My wife. Ex, I mean. I used to be married. Not now. I'm not a cheater." Why the fuck had he blurted that out?

From his outpost in the rickety chair he'd reoccupied, Ransom's sharp inhalation rang through the room. Was it that hard to believe? Or simply shocking that he'd admitted it to Rivet when he'd never come clean to

Ransom, despite the guy's periodic line of similar questioning.

"What happened?" Her gentle, empathetic probes did something to him. Made him want to tell her despite years of locking his pain away.

It could be like some form of confession, clearing the air and his conscience just in case he didn't have a lot of time left. Or it could be stupid to share how his mistakes had led him to this final showdown.

Rivet wasn't going to let him off the hook so easily.

"You got divorced because of Wildfire? Is your ex a club whore?" She lost most of her rosy glow as blood drained from her face. "I don't know her, do I? What's stopping her from ratting you out to Angus?"

Ransom leaned forward, putting his elbows on his knees as he stared at Levi, who flopped to his back and glared at the water spots on the shitty ceiling tiles, which drooped over their heads. They were as likely to come crashing down as the web of lies and subterfuge they'd been weaving for too long already.

He had to make Rivet, and Ransom, understand everything that was at stake. They had to get in, get the info Jordan needed, and get the fuck out before things collapsed, burying them all alive.

Well, Rivet and Ransom anyway. He didn't care much about what happened to himself as long as the other two made it out alive. Unlike his wife.

"No, Laurel can't talk. She's dead." So much for the relaxation that had swept over him with his orgasm. It vanished the instant he uttered her name, replaced by guilt and despair and self-loathing.

"Shit. I'm sorry." Rivet put her hand on his chest and cuddled closer to him, infusing him with her heat.

While he should have gotten up and paced, suddenly he felt too weary to resist the comfort she offered. Besides, there wasn't anywhere to go in this shithole. So he shifted, joining her under the covers and gathering her close to his heart like he'd never be able to do with Laurel again.

They hadn't been right for each other. But they'd been too young and eager to realize they were actually in love with the idea of falling in love and not necessarily each other.

Levi glanced at Ransom. The guy's eyes opened wide and his eyebrows climbed his craggy forehead as Levi settled in. So what? Even he needed a break sometime, and they all knew that's what this was—the calm before the shit-storm. With one night of cathartic therapy—their sexual release coupled with talking shit through—he might be able to last long enough to finish what they'd started before he lost his mind completely.

Rivet drew his attention back to her with a quiet acceptance he certainly hadn't earned.

"There are so many things about you I never guessed. Makes it kind of hard to know what's real and what's not." She drew a never-ending figure eight on the side of his neck, lulling him. "I think I've been caught up in lies so long now, my whole life honestly, that I've learned not to trust anything. Tell me this isn't one of those times where I should be skeptical."

"Oh, you definitely should be. But not about what we did together. I promise you that what we shared tonight was genuine. If I even know who I am anymore, you had every bit of the real me just now." Levi sighed.

"That's what she said." Rivet snorted softly, making him chuckle too despite the solemn note in the stale air, then closed her eyes. Fighting to stay alert and awake, she was losing the battle. "Okay, that's enough for me."

"You going to get some sleep, too?" Levi asked Ransom, though he was too damn selfish to offer to let go of Rivet in order to take the first shift on watch.

It had been years since he'd drifted off in a lover's arms. And though he hadn't thought that was something he wanted ever again, there he was, reluctant to sacrifice the one chance he'd have to experience it for probably as long. Maybe ever.

"I'm good." Ransom scanned Levi and Rivet. "You two should rest, though. Tomorrow isn't going to be fun for anyone."

Rivet grunted at that and nuzzled her face into the crook of Levi's shoulder. For a few moments they were still. He imagined his mind might quiet enough for him to doze off in an hour or two.

Did it make any sense that he sort of wished they hadn't stopped talking? Now that they'd taken a break and his emotions had receded enough to allow him to think clearly again, it seemed impossible to dive back into the heavy topic they'd been flirting with.

"So you're really not going to tell me what happened to Laurel?" Rivet wondered. He should have realized she wouldn't let it go so easily.

"I think we've had enough bedtime stories for one night, don't you?" Levi asked.

"No," both Rivet and Ransom said in unison.

Great, that was just what he needed. To be outvoted and ganged up on all the damn time.

"Good luck, Rivet. I've been trying to get him to tell me that for years now." Ransom grimaced. For the first time Levi realized that his own shame might have been hurting the other guy. At the very least, it was unbalanced and unfair since he knew every fact about the very public case that had landed Ransom in jail before he'd gotten his sentence converted by agreeing to his current position. "And when I tried to research it I didn't get very far. Someone's scrubbed his records. Who knows if Levi is even his real name?"

"For fuck's sake, Ransom. You know me. That's what counts. And it's not that I don't trust you or some shit." Levi frowned at Ransom. Hell, they'd relied on each other for so long now, the other guy was an extension of him. "It's just...stuff I'd rather not think about, never mind discuss."

"What could be so horrible to tell *me*?" Ransom crossed his arms. "Or have you forgotten that I murdered someone, for Christ's sake? How could it be worse than that?"

To her credit, Rivet didn't gasp or recoil, though she stiffened against Levi. He might as well come clean too. So that she understood he wasn't someone to have foolish feelings for. Especially after how close they'd been earlier, it was important that they make a clean break from this moment forward.

"Because the person who died because of me was someone I loved. Someone I should have protected, yet didn't, like you did. My goddamned wife." Levi couldn't say more than that. Acid bubbled up in his esophagus. Fuck, he shouldn't have eaten so much pizza then shaken it around with his fucking.

If Laurel could see him now, she wouldn't recognize the man he'd become. Getting off without emotion, using his partners purely for sexual satisfaction, putting everyone at risk for his own selfish needs, obliterating the sensitive side of himself in favor of cold practicalities. Well, okay, she might have been too familiar with that last bit.

Fuck.

When Rivet stirred as if she was going to hug him or something equally affectionate, he knew he had to cut things off right there. Fucking was one thing. More than that was impossible. Irresponsible. For him. Forever.

He rolled onto his side, facing away from her, though refusing to look Ransom in the eye either, and drew the covers up to his neck. Not because the hotel was drafty as fuck either.

"She overdosed. On fentanyl-laced heroin provided to the local dealers by Wildfire, okay?"

"How is that your fault?" Rivet squeezed him from behind. "Addiction is a horrible illness. I'm assuming you didn't shoot it into her arm for her."

"Might as well have." Hatred—for himself as well as the outlaws who'd sold Laurel more than she bargained for—flashed through him, balling his fists and clenching his teeth. "She was clean for three years before I told her I was bisexual and that I wondered if she'd be up for a night of experimenting with me and a friend of mine."

"Ah, fuck." Ransom groaned. "I hope tonight didn't trigger any bad memories for you."

"Worse. I didn't think about it until just now."

Laurel's face, and the disapproving, hurt—no, *betrayed* —expression that had crossed it right before she locked herself in their tiny apartment bathroom and sobbed for hours flashed through his mind.

"I'd met her when I was just a rookie cop and she was on probation, getting her act together. I was so proud of her for fighting that hard. Loved her for how strong and resilient she was. And I ruined it all. Crushed her. I knew she was delicate. I shouldn't have told her the truth. Or better yet, I shouldn't have gotten tangled up with her in the first place. It was inevitable that I was going to disappoint her."

Rivet cursed and shook him then. "You can't help how you are any more than she could. You were honest with her, didn't break your vows, and definitely are not responsible for her decisions."

He made some noncommittal sound that was acknowledgement yet not agreement.

Then he looked to Ransom, expecting to see censure in the other man's eyes. Hell, he'd killed a man to protect his sister, and here Levi had been the driving force behind his wife's death.

Ransom would never respect him again. That was fine if it meant he wouldn't take any risks to save Levi's hide once they rejoined Wildfire. Ransom had been locked up for his actions, but what Levi had done was far worse.

Except what he saw in Ransom's warm whiskey-colored stare was compassion. And understanding. He'd lost a lot too in his lifetime. Everything. "Sometimes our actions have unintended consequences. That's a tragedy. But you said it yourself. I *know* you. You're a good man, Levi, regardless of what you've endured. The three of us are survivors. Maybe we should stop hating ourselves for that."

Levi was shaken to his core that Ransom got it. Got him.

So at first he didn't notice Rivet's fingers were trembling on his arm. Her uneven breaths buffeted the nape of his neck. Oh shit, was she crying?

He rolled to face her, which also saved him from

accepting Ransom's impossible challenge. Crystalline moisture pooled in the corner of her wide eyes.

"He's right, you know. You're not responsible for your mother's choices. She was grown, you weren't." Levi brushed his thumb over her cheekbone.

"Does knowing any of that make it hurt less?" she whispered.

No. No, it didn't.

"Nah. But being inside you did, for a little while." Unfortunately, it had been a temporary reprieve. "Will it help if I hold you tonight?"

Rivet nodded. She crushed them together and he would have been lying if he said that consoling her didn't have some similar effect on himself. He only wished Ransom would join them. But when he looked over his shoulder, the other guy had returned to staring blankly out the crusty window.

Levi's legs tangled with Rivet's much more slender ones, finding that they fit together really well. So well that neither of them felt the need to disturb what little harmony they had managed to find in each other's arms by rehashing more of their traumatic pasts.

The rest of Levi's night was restless, though somewhere in the back of his mind he realized Ransom never roused him for a turn on watch. Rivet either. She snored and snuffled adorably next to him every time he surfaced from a nightmare about Laurel, foaming at the mouth where she'd died in that alley, haunting him for failing her.

Until a loud rumble was followed by a string of bangs on the door, startling him awake. "Hey, what the fuck are you guys doing in there? Open up before we bust this piece of shit down. Angus told us to bring you in and I'm not risking my nuts by taking any longer than absolutely necessary. Hurry your asses up."

Levi glanced down at Rivet, still tucked into his embrace. Her eyes flew open, and instead of a sleepy sexiness, they were brimming with abject terror. She hissed, "Let go!"

So he did. But was it too late?

He should have known he was bad for her. For Ransom. For anyone.

Levi shoved her away.

10

If Ransom had been Jordan or even Levi, he'd have fired himself right then. Stopping there would be too kind. He should be locked in the deepest, darkest cell in jail before the key was melted down, trapping him forever. He was a danger to those he cared about, and everyone who relied on him. He shouldn't be trusted, especially not with anyone else's wellbeing.

He'd failed Levi and Rivet.

How the fuck had all three of them drifted off at the same time and been knocked out so hard that the ruckus of Wildfire approaching hadn't even roused them? His fault. He hadn't had the heart to wake either Levi or Rivet when they were both clearly exhausted by their physical and emotional outpouring. He'd thought he was doing them a favor by letting them take it easy while he stayed on guard since they only had one night of the ceasefire left before they walked back into the Wildfire of hell.

His mistake. This was only going to work if they were a team and relied on each other. But not *too* much.

He'd been selfish. Let himself sneak a taste of what they'd enjoyed together.

Ransom had known better than to give in to their seduction. But he was weak. Always had been. And now they were going to pay for his softness. This could never happen again.

He dashed to the bed, scooped his hands under Rivet's petite frame, and practically tossed her from the center of the bed toward the bathroom. Levi dove for the floor, then lobbed her binders in the same direction.

She caught them midair before bolting for the bathroom, her slender bare back a flash of pale white skin interrupted only by the marks Levi had left there. Both Ransom and Levi frantically scanned the room, looking for anything out of place or any clues that would give them—Rivet especially—away.

Ransom yanked the comforter and one of the pillows from the bed, then threw them on the floor to make it appear as if Levi hadn't indulged in a night of full body contact with Rivet, his arm slung over her as if he could shelter her from what was coming.

That wouldn't fly with these guys. Especially since Rivet's safety depended on them continuing to believe she was the young, straight man they thought she was. And if they did that, they certainly weren't going to be okay with the idea of their brothers getting it on together.

Being different wasn't really an option at Wildfire.

At the intersection of where Ransom was satisfied they'd covered their asses and how long he reasonably thought he could delay the bastards pounding on their cheap door, he looked to Levi, who nodded. So Ransom yanked the thing open.

He didn't have to act annoyed when he grumbled,

"What the hell are you doing here so early? And why are you so fucking loud?"

"Ah, had a wild one last night, huh?" Three guys, who were notorious partiers themselves, like most of the gang at Wildfire, cracked up.

They *had* indulged. Just not in the vices the club guys thought. Their shenanigans had been a fuck-ton more fun than getting hammered or high, and more dangerous, too.

God, it had been forever since Ransom had touched a woman. Sure, there were plenty of club whores he could have picked from, but he sort of insisted his women be willing, and he didn't figure fucking because you had no other option counted.

Especially now that he knew the full story about Levi and the demons that plagued him—as well as Rivet and the damage it had done to her when Wildfire had stolen her mother—he would never take advantage of the women who traded sex for drugs or the warped sense of security that came from hiding in the shadow of fear the motorcycle club cast all around it. To Levi, every one of them were Laurel. Ransom could see that now. No wonder his partner had shown absolutely no interest in them, never once been tempted when the club whores threw themselves at him, although he'd told Ransom he was bisexual and not only attracted to men.

To be honest, Ransom simply hadn't believed it. Now he did. He'd seen the proof the night before.

He had gotten used to spying on illicit affairs during his time in prison. There hadn't been a lot of ways to avoid it. Hell, he'd even gotten used to accepting offers for BJs from some men when he was desperate for human interaction himself.

But watching Levi fuck Rivet had done things to him. Filthy things. Incredible things.

Things that could never happen again.

"Yeah, we had a hell of a night. Figured we should live it up before coming home with bad news." He blocked as much of the entry for as long as possible, pretending to be sluggish with the hangover their visitors expected. "Good to see you too, Red."

The ginger grimaced. "Yeah, well, you should think about how fucking temperamental Angus is before you decide that. Getting locked up might have been better than what he has in store for you three."

"I bet. Losing Clive is a big blow." Ransom cheered inside even if he acted grim. Wildfire's now-ex sergeant-at-arms had been apprehended back in Middletown, thanks in large part to Rivet, who had lured him into the open. The asshole was a key witness in the RICO case they were building against his old president.

"Clive's about to be *lost* all right." The guy spit on the ground. "He's got to know he's done for, right? If it was me, I'd off myself and save Angus the trouble."

Ransom figured the guy was under close watch in solitary so he didn't do just that. Not to mention protecting him from anyone else Angus might have paid to do the job for him. "He fought them, but..." He shook his head.

From behind Red, one of the other guys, a tall, lanky dude everyone called Stix, groaned. "Might as well be dead."

"That's why we got the fuck out of there before we could join him." Ransom didn't have to fake his horror at that idea. Going back to prison wasn't an option. He'd do exactly like Red said if it came down to it. He couldn't survive locked up. It had nearly driven him insane. Why the fuck else would he have allowed himself to get caught up in all this bullshit?

"Where's Rivet?" Red craned his neck to peer around Ransom. Of course his too-loud voice carried just fine through the paper-thin walls of the roach motel.

"Can't a guy take a shit in peace?" Rivet shouted from inside the tiny bathroom, making their welcoming party crack up. Her outburst also guaranteed no one would be poking their head in before she was ready to come out. She was clever and a quick thinker. He admired that about her. She had balls of absolute steel too, to have been playing this game on her own. At least he'd always had Levi to watch his back and vice versa.

"Probably means he's rubbing one out since he's too shy to score any pussy." Stix shook his head as if he couldn't understand why someone wouldn't indulge in one of the primary club benefits. Even prospects got their fair share. "We ain't got time for that. I'm not winding up on Angus's bad side."

"Does he have a good side?" Levi grumbled, then shouted over his shoulder, "Rivet, hurry the hell up! We're leaving."

"Yeah, yeah. Coming."

Red snorted at that. Seconds later, Rivet smashed the bathroom door into the wall and let the *whoosh* of the flushing toilet carry through the room.

"Hey. I figured we'd seen the last of you." Red lifted his chin at Rivet in some kind of nod of respect.

"You thought I quit the club? Fuck you, Red. I'm no pussy." Rivet wasn't hard to take seriously when she yanked her sleeves up as if preparing to settle things like most of the brothers would after an insult. Even her walk was different as she approached, legs spread and knees bent in the perfect imitation of a cocky biker.

"Good to know. But we'll see what tune you're singing after you talk to Angus." Red winced.

"How worried should I be?" Ransom asked. This was their last chance to change their course if the Wildfire president was set on eliminating them for their involvement in the supposed debacle that had landed Clive in prison and gotten Angus no closer to having his son and heir back in the club ranks.

"Depends on how much you enjoy having your head attached to your neck or your dick fully functional." Red shrugged. "I'm just glad I'm not you guys."

Stix leaned in, a leer plastered on his leathery face. "Is it true Walker knocked Joy up finally? And that Dane is fine with it?"

"Appears so." Ransom nodded. "Nothing we said had any effect. They're not coming back unless it's by force, and even I'm not stupid enough to try that outright."

"Too bad." Red huffed. "Things might be better around here with a change of the guard, if you know what I mean."

Ransom's brow rose. It must be getting bad if the guys were willing to whisper treason, even on the sly and to their most trusted comrades. Angus was spiraling out of control. And they were going to go down with him if they didn't put a stop to it.

This could be good news for him, Levi, and Rivet.

As the president of the motorcycle club, Angus had absolute authority and was also the biggest target around. If they could get guys to start taking pot shots from within the organization in addition to making him vulnerable to his enemies in rival clubs, Levi and Rivet could put this behind them and get back to a normal, safe, happy life.

After what Ransom had seen the night before, he guessed they might even want to try doing that together.

On the other hand, he had done horrible stuff. He didn't deserve what was waiting for Rivet on the other side of this shit show or even what could be in store for Levi too, if he didn't get too caught up. Ransom had already seen the guy slide deeper into the darkness they'd submerged themselves in. He swore he wouldn't let that happen to his friend.

Friend. Was that was Levi was, or was it more than that? More than fuck buddies even.

It was probably for the best if Rivet took that spot from him. No way could he let what they'd done the night before, or in the months previous, happen again. Not even that much and definitely not more. Despite what his body craved.

His gaze flicked to her, looking every bit the dude he'd thought she was until recently. His dick stirred. Maybe he wasn't quite as straight as he'd always assumed. It wouldn't be the only thing he'd been mistaken about. He was capable of a lot of things he hadn't realized when he'd been naive and the world had made sense.

Whatever she saw in his stare must have freaked her out. She knew they'd pushed their luck and they couldn't afford to keep doing it now.

"We better get the fuck out of here if you don't want to smell what I just dropped in there. Goddamn beer shits." She shoved past Levi and Ransom, and crashed through the gaggle of bikers waiting beyond without hesitation. And just like that, Rivet was back in the game.

So Ransom followed. Like hell would he leave her or Levi to face this evil alone.

"There's only one bed in this shithole?" Red asked as if he'd just realized it. The guys looked around like another one would pop out of the crusty carpet and magically appear. "What'd you do, share it? You fags."

Ransom gave him the finger and shoved him for good measure. He wasn't about to let them talk shit about Levi, even if they didn't actually think he was gay or bisexual. "Yeah right. That's why my back's practically broken from sleeping in those chairs. What'd you come here for? To bust our balls or to welcome us home?"

"We made the prospect take the floor, bugs and all. I'm not in the mood for dumb shit," Levi growled as he too plowed through Red and his guys on his way to his bike.

Ransom tossed the room keys onto the bed, then ushered Red, Stix, and their buddy out the door, locking it behind them. Together, they ambled toward the six gleaming motorcycles waiting for them to ride straight into the bowels of hell together.

"I'm not sure if we'll be throwing a party or kicking some ass. Don't hate us if he makes us teach you a lesson. With Clive gone, someone's going to have to do his dirty work." Red continued asking a million questions about what exactly had gone down, none of which Ransom felt like answering.

So instead he said, "Why don't we save the play by play for Angus?"

Red nodded. "Let's go."

One by one, they peeled out of the lot, zooming down the rural street with a roar that was sure to make old ladies shake their fists and young men envious. Falling into formation, Ransom was careful not to stick too close to Rivet or Levi. He didn't want anyone getting exactly the right idea about them.

The distance between them felt astronomical compared to the intimacy they'd shared for one special night in a roach motel. An unlikely sanctuary, but one he was sure they were going to miss every minute between now and when things came to a head.

He vowed right then and there, as he gripped the handlebars and reveled in the wind buffeting his face, that he would shield Levi and Rivet from the worst of what was to come. This wasn't about putting Angus away in exchange for his own freedom anymore. It was about saving two decent people in the hopes that it might even the scales for what he'd done before.

Adrenaline, bad decisions, and a lifetime of repercussions. Ransom had committed the ultimate sin. The mack daddy of them all. He'd taken someone's life. A judge and jury had ruled that being threatened hadn't been a good enough reason to protect his little sister, because she'd been in the wrong to begin with.

Of course he hadn't known that. And even if he had, what else could he have done? Watched her be killed right in front of his eyes? No, he'd reacted on instinct and ended up stealing someone else's future.

The memory of his victim's mother and her tearful plea in the courtroom for him to pay for what he'd stolen from her and the rest of her family played on constant repeat in his mind.

He deserved the worst.

He deserved to die for what he'd done.

Ransom tried not to think like that, but in the darkest hours of the night, it was all he could dwell on. Things wouldn't be right until he'd paid for what he'd done because being sorry about it clearly wouldn't bring the dead man back or alleviate his family's grief. He knew that for sure, because he'd regretted it every moment since it had happened.

Levi and Rivet deserved better. And they definitely shouldn't soil themselves with his taint.

They'd gone temporarily insane, all three of them. This could never happen again.

Especially not now that they were headed straight into the source of the flames. Because if they weren't careful, they would get fried. Only he deserved that fate.

Ransom swore then and there that he'd do anything it took to get Levi and Rivet out of this mess alive so they had a chance at being happy...together.

That was probably his best chance at atoning for his offenses.

Even the worst one.

11

Rivet didn't immediately climb from her bike after they pulled into the lot where the Wildfire clubhouse sat, attached to the back of the garage where she was a mechanic for Angus. Of course the legit business was primarily a front for his racketeering nonsense, but they did actual repairs there.

At least she did. Even under these circumstances, she took pride in her workmanship. Anything less than her best would have been an insult to her grandfather and the effort he'd expended to teach her everything he'd known.

Rivet stared at the cinderblocks, painted matte black with vivid, glossy flames on them, and wondered how it could be so similar to and yet nothing like Hot Rides and their sister shop Hot Rods. Ambition and dedication could take an organization in two vastly different directions depending on the morals and guidance of their leadership, she supposed.

She'd lived in this twisted version of reality for so long she'd almost forgotten what things should be like. And now that she'd been reminded that there was still goodness and light out there, not to mention experiencing an epic night of pleasure with Levi and Ransom, it made the stakes that much higher.

Because suddenly she cared not only about bringing Angus to justice, but about making it out of this mess alive, whole, and able to pursue something like she'd had if only for that single glorious moment.

If Levi or Ransom felt the same, though, she had no clue.

They were pretty fucking decent actors. She had never suspected they were some kind of cops before. If she didn't know it for certain now, she still wouldn't have guessed it. They'd all but ignored her since the other Wildfire members had discovered them, not even staying near her in the formation of riders as they'd grown ever closer to Wildfire's stronghold.

Jordan's plan had worked a little too well. The club members had found them much sooner than she'd anticipated. It had taken miles and miles of riding on the open highway before her heart rate had returned to normal after nearly being busted in bed, naked, with Levi while Ransom looked on.

That would have put a quick end to her ruse. And likely gotten her gang raped while they were at it. She would have been lucky if they'd simply killed her instead of making her suffer their brutality first. She wouldn't have lasted more than an hour as one of the club whores, and though she hadn't told Levi about it—especially once she'd learned about the fate of his poor ex-wife—she kept a capsule of botulinum toxin she'd bought off some shady-as-fuck internet site tucked into her pocket at all times.

She wasn't sure if the shit was real, or if it would work

as advertised, but it gave her the courage to face Wildfire, knowing that she would have an out if she needed it. Even if it meant a one-way ticket to hell, it would be better than some of the fates she could imagine at the club's hands.

Rivet shivered despite the sunshine making the late winter day warmer than it had been for a while. Spring was coming, though she had a hard time imagining the world turning green and fresh and new while she stared at the desolate Wildfire den. On one side, a mural depicted a forest fire, the sweeping inferno chasing even the fiercest animals, making them flee or be devoured. The macabre scene, including bears, wolves, and bobcats, their faces twisted in grotesque fear and suffering, was intended to intimidate their enemies.

It was working right then. She wasn't anywhere near as powerful as one of those creatures. She was merely a woman with a hell of a grudge. What chance did she stand against them?

Too late to worry about that now.

"Come on," Ransom barked from his place at the head of the pack, heading straight to the heart of evil—Angus's office. Her presence was required. It was time to see if her risky maneuver had paid off.

She'd left Wildfire to find her sister, to relay important information, and ask for help—which she'd received in the form of Levi and Ransom, plus the rest of Jordan's resources—so that she could take her fight to the next level. That part of her plan had been wildly successful. Now all she had to do was convince Angus she'd really been trying to talk his errant son and stepdaughter into returning to the fold, bringing their newborn daughter along for the ride.

Like she would ever put her family in danger now that they'd escaped.

Rivet kept her head down like the good little prospect she supposedly was and jogged to keep up with the rest of the gang. After everything she'd done to avoid notice and fly under the radar until now, it felt odd to be the focus of any attention.

She was going to have to get used to it. Because that was her alibi.

According to the scenario they'd laid out, she'd vanished to try to drag Joy back and gain Angus's favor, which also meant she was a failure as well as a soldier who'd gone temporarily rogue—even if it was in an attempt to demonstrate her dedication and ambition.

Rivet jammed her hands in her hoodie pouch pocket so no one could see how sweaty and unsteady they were. Without thought, she lifted them an inch or so, keeping the front of the material from stretching across her chest, highlighting the smothered swells of her breasts.

She had to be extra careful since staring at Levi and Ransom's tight asses in front of her was enough to trigger her damn hormones and make her nipples ache and harden. Even now, she had to fight her attraction to them. It had been bad enough when she'd had a crush on Levi. With Ransom added to the mix, it was twice the distractions and double the risk.

Focus!

As they approached, the corrugated metal of the reinforced door slid open with a clang. The noise it made when it shut was deafening. It shook every bone in her body while her eyes adjusted to the dark and smoky interior of the clubhouse.

The main area was made up of busted and worn black

leather couches, a glossy black painted cement floor with occasional red exterior-grade rugs. Skulls, old bike parts, and chrome lent garish accents to the place. Loud music swirled around a fully stocked bar, complete with drugs in hidden safes to go with the booze. Club whores and old ladies paraded around in barely enough leather and strategically ripped jean shorts to cover the bare essentials. Sometimes not even that.

The entire place reeked of sex, drugs, and terrible decisions.

Everything was exactly how she'd left it. Including the guarded metal door behind them.

They were committed now. Trapped.

Rivet stared at her boots to avoid glancing at Ransom and Levi. Or worse, to allow anyone else to glimpse the disgust that washed over her every time she considered this was what her own mother had sacrificed their time together for. What the fuck?

She could easily imagine Angus sprawled on one of the couches, getting a BJ right there like he was some sort of a king instead of a villain. Forcing her mother to kneel and serve him where everyone could watch to keep her place in the ranks. Lower than any of the men in the club but the highest of all the women around.

Not exactly what Rivet would consider a win.

What was wrong with her that her mother had chosen this instead of her own flesh and blood? Rivet froze as doubt and regret swamped her. When the rest of the guys headed for Angus's office, she fell behind.

"Go ahead." Red shoved her in the center of her back, forcing her to bound forward or fall on her face. "If you're going to be man enough to run off on your own, you can be man enough to face the consequences."

Truth be told, Rivet wasn't man enough for anything. That didn't mean she wasn't strong. She thought of her mother and how the woman had challenged Angus, how she'd exerted her influence over him in subtle and cunning ways, methods far more effective than his blunt ones.

That was what she had to do, too. Only she'd do it better.

Because Rivet had no love for that motherfucker.

That's where her mother had gone wrong. Rivet sure as fuck wasn't going to make the same mistake. She saw him for the vile despot he was.

Levi opened the door to Angus's office. He ushered her and Ransom inside. The other three men who'd escorted them back disappeared into the depths of the club faster than she would have imagined possible when their legs had to be at least as stiff as hers from the ride.

Probably the only smart thing they'd done lately. Better to be as far away as possible from the president when he lost his shit.

Too bad she was about to be in the direct line of fire.

"Well, look who's home." Angus had his back to them. The ultimate show of power. Here, in his lair, he was confident they couldn't stab him between his shoulder blades or put a bullet through his brain. It was a clear signal. He had absolute control here.

If Rivet had something more than her pocketknife handy, she would have attempted to assassinate him. Too bad that would mean they'd be dead before they could leave the clubhouse. Nah, they wouldn't even make it out of this room.

And while she didn't give much of a shit about her

own fate, she suddenly cared more than she'd like to admit about Levi's and Ransom's.

Damn it.

Maybe having them on her side would make things harder instead of easier.

None of them were dumb enough to speak up without being asked a direct question, so they fell into a line, shoulder to shoulder, Ransom and Levi flanking her. It would look to Angus like they were bringing her in, when she knew it was the tiniest bit of protection they could give her.

Damn, they were chivalrous, even if they couldn't show it or didn't realize it themselves.

Angus had his hands clasped in the small of his back, a black T-shirt stretched across his fit body. It would be appropriate if he were an ogre, as ugly on the outside as he was on the inside. But no, like his son Walker, he was a hell of a specimen. At least her mom had good taste in that regard.

He was tall, built, and sexy even before the allure of his clout was factored in. Tattoos sleeved his arms and wound around his neck. Heavy silver rings decorated most of his fingers and thick chains wrapped his wrists, neck, and even draped from his belt loop.

A lit cigar gave off pungent smoke, which curled in the air above his obsidian desk, reminding her of a translucent gray poison serpent.

"Strip," he commanded, catching her off guard.

Did he know? Was she about to face her worst nightmares? Rivet fingered the capsule in her pocket and pulled her tongue back to allow spit to gather in her mouth.

Ransom tensed and Levi cut his gaze to her from beneath his lowered blond lashes.

"I mean, I've been hitting the gym for a while now, but I didn't think you'd noticed," Levi joked, although this was no time to antagonize Angus. He was trying to divert attention from her, and it was working.

The man whipped around, his dark, dead eyes narrowing even as his glare snapped to Levi. "Don't act like you're shy all of a sudden. That's Rivet's thing. Afraid to show me you're not wearing a wire?"

"Is that even how technology works these days?" Ransom grinned. "Come on, pres. We can do better than that."

They could? Rivet thought of the binders beneath her clothes and how sunk she'd be if Angus revealed them now.

"I'm not a man who takes things on faith. You've been gone too long. And around too many cops for my liking. How do I know you're not working with them?" He crossed his arms, making his chest seem even burlier than it was.

"Because you can scan us with this..." Ransom reached into his pocket and drew out the bug-detection device Jordan had given them. He'd said it was a loaner from his friend JRad, some super security-freak programmer who worked for a division of the OHPD affectionately referred to as the Men in Blue.

Son of a bitch! That was one of the things they'd need most if they were going to have any chance of communicating between them without getting caught.

Still, if it was get busted now or down the road, she'd defer being discovered as long as possible.

"What's that?" Angus stepped closer, making Rivet's skin crawl.

"Consider it a gift." Ransom grinned. "I stole it out of the tech van the cops left parked by the diner where they cornered us."

"So you traded this piece of shit for Clive?" Angus snatched the device from Ransom, wiping the faux-smirk from his face, then marched back to his desk. He flipped it around in his hand as he crossed the space with crisp, efficient strides. The top center drawer opened with a metallic hiss so he could withdraw something from inside. Whatever it was, his fingertips obscured it completely. It was tiny, light, and fragile.

None of them were stupid enough to speak.

Angus lifted his face to glare at them. "Hard to imagine any piece of hardware being a more valuable resource than my sergeant-at-arms. Why the fuck didn't you protect *him*?"

"Rivet was playing it cool. Acting harmless while he spoke with Joy. Ransom was guarding the rear exit so we had an escape path," Levi answered for them.

"And you?" Angus asked, his head tipping slightly.

"I had to choose between protecting Walker or Clive." Levi shrugged.

"Then you should have let my son suffer the consequences of leaving the security of Wildfire behind." Angus sneered, making Rivet aware of just how cruel he could be. Who would say that about their own child? Especially as good a man as Walker. Her mother and Angus really had been a matched set. "He's a traitor. Dead to me, anyway. Clive has only ever been loyal, even though he's obviously never been strong enough to make the cut. Fuck it. They're both worthless."

For one split second, Angus seemed weary.

Then he recovered, straightening before he waved the device Ransom had given him over whatever he'd placed on the surface of his desk. A shrill beep broadcast through the room, startling her and piercing her eardrums. "Well, fuck. I paid nearly five grand for that piece of shit. It's supposed to be undetectable."

Angus brought his fist down and smashed the bug. At least Rivet knew what to be on the lookout for when they searched their apartments later.

They'd have to settle for doing it the old-fashioned way. If they made it out of here alive.

Angus's temper kept rising. And they were the only targets in range.

He stormed over to them, his face reddening despite his outward calm.

Instead of decking them, or slipping a switchblade between their ribs, or whatever other terrifying and cruel fates he could cook up, Angus lashed out with the sweeper in his hand and waved it along all of Ransom's extremities and core before moving on to Levi.

Then it was her turn.

Rivet refused to allow herself to cow before him. She met his stare as he guided the device around her body, thankfully not close enough to notice her camouflaged curves. She owed Ransom one already. If Angus had seen her binders, she'd have been tossed into the clubhouse living area and descended on by a pack of bikers, who wouldn't take kindly to being duped.

He took his time as if testing her, to see if she would flinch.

She didn't.

"Have a nice vacation?" Angus asked, clearly fuming beneath his false-friend tone.

"It didn't go quite like I hoped. I was close, though," Rivet grumbled, playing the part of a rookie who'd overreached. "I nearly had Joy convinced that coming here would be best for her baby before Clive showed up and scared her right back into Walker and Dane's arms. And then those fucking cops so rudely interrupted. Everything went to hell after that."

She intentionally didn't say sorry. Because Wildfire never showed weakness. Not even, or maybe not especially, to their leader.

"You have more balls than I thought." Angus studying her so intently, and from so close by made her skin crawl. She clamped down on the urge to fidget or shudder. "It's a decent approach to fly under the radar like that. So I'm thinking you're smarter than I gave you credit for too. I'll have to use you more often."

"Thanks." Rivet beamed, though it was only because Angus was going to give her a chance to get close to him again and not because she relished the thought of doing his dirty work.

"But next time you wander off without my permission, I won't be so fucking nice about it." He backhanded her, making her ears ring as he wiped her grin off her face.

She dropped to her knees, one hand flying out at the last second to keep her from smacking flat onto the floor. Her tongue swiped around her mouth, verifying her teeth remained in place even if the front lower one seemed like it might have been chipped by one of Angus's chunky silver rings.

In her peripheral vision, she saw Levi's and Ransom's

legs tense, their calves bulging in their faded jeans. Thankfully, neither of them budged. Doing so would have blown their cover for sure. Most established members of the club wouldn't give a shit if a junior member was taught a lesson. Hell, they'd all lived through it themselves. Felt it was a rite of passage and totally normal.

For the guys' sakes more than her own, she shook her head and blinked until she stopped seeing double, then got to her feet, spitting blood onto the floor when it curdled her taste buds with a metallic tang.

Angus was there, staring down at her with a smirk on his face. "I underestimated you, Rivet."

Well, shit. That wasn't really what she'd planned, but good enough. She didn't dare speak. Not out of deference to him, like he probably thought, but to keep her howl of indignation locked inside and to prevent herself from telling him what a sack of shit she really thought he was. The defiance in her stare must have come across as fortitude since he spared her another blow.

"And since I did, I'm going to insist these two babysit you for a while. Just in case there was more happening on your field trip than you're letting on." Angus turned toward Ransom and Levi. "Since you didn't manage to bring back Clive or Joy or Walker or even Dane, for that matter, you can find room in your apartment for Rivet to bunk with you."

"You want us to live together?" Ransom cut his eyes to Angus. Was he acting pissed that they'd have to share space with her or was he really unhappy about being in close quarters with her again. She couldn't say if she was relieved or dreading it herself. None of their personal feelings mattered, though. What Angus ordered went. "Why?"

"I want to know if Walker, Joy, or Dane, or the fucking cops, anyone at all, reaches out to our little weasel here." Angus jabbed a finger in her direction. "Besides, I already gave his place over the garage to the new apprentice I brought in to fill his sudden vacancy at the shop."

"What?" Rivet didn't dare rip him, though she wanted to. Thank God she hadn't left anything incriminating in the drafty old flat.

"Didn't think I'd ever see you again." Angus smiled then and shrugged. "You've impressed me, Rivet. That's why I'm promoting you. To supervisor at the garage and a full member. Get that prospect patch off your cut."

"Seriously?" That genuinely surprised her. She'd assumed he'd be pissed she fucked up, not impressed that she'd tried at all. This would give her a lot more leeway, and the ability to sneak around unguarded most times. Unless it was by Ransom and Levi, which hardly counted. This couldn't have worked out better.

"I didn't think you had what it took to be a full Wildfire member, but I see I was wrong about you." He nodded as if he was bestowing some great honor on her. In his world, he was. That made her feel slimy, but she'd live. "Have Red give you a member patch before you leave tonight."

Of course, it didn't really serve her purposes to increase his estimation of her, but it was what it was. And if it gave her a reason to bunk with Levi and Ransom, she wasn't going to be too sad about the tradeoff. Overall, this could be good news for their partnership.

She didn't want to show it, though. So she smothered her grin and hoped it came out more like a wry smile when she said, "Thank you, president."

"Hey, Rivet."

"Yeah?" she asked, thinking to herself how glorious it would be when she finally made him pay for how he'd mistreated every person around him for years.

"Get your ass back to work. I'm giving you a raise because I expect you to be more useful now that I know what you're capable of." Angus bared his teeth in a facsimile of a smile. "And there are no demotions around here. Only failures."

"Don't worry about that." She had to curl her fingers into her palm to resist giving him the finger. She wasn't going to bomb her mission, though he might wish she had someday. "I can take care of my own shit."

"I see that." He nodded. "Interesting. Now get the fuck out of here. All three of you."

12

The front door of their apartment opened, making Levi whip his head in that direction. He relaxed when Rivet came through it, and stripped off her cut. She never wore it a moment longer than necessary and refused to treat it with respect. The leather crinkled as she tossed it on the ground near the mat they kept their shoes on.

He figured her micro-rebellion was unlikely to bite them in the ass since they only ever associated with other members at the clubhouse, not in their own space. Angus preferred it that way so he could keep an eye on everyone and make sure they weren't getting up to any trouble that could lead to a revolt.

Rivet looked cute as always, though beat—with ever-darkening circles under her eyes—as she bent over to untie and loosen the laces on her tall black boots before toeing them off. Carefully, she set her helmet on the shelf.

"How was work?"

"Fine." She shrugged. "Actually got to work on some cool bikes today. Took my mind off stuff for a few hours."

Instantly, he relaxed. At least for one more night, everything was okay. They'd survived another day undercover and now they could relax together until they had to do it again the next morning.

At first, Levi had thought living with Rivet and Ransom would be pure torture. *Two* of the most alluring, tempting people he'd ever met under one roof and he couldn't touch either of them, unless they could guarantee they'd be better at staying focused than they had been the last time they'd fooled around.

Yeah, not happening.

But now he couldn't deny he was getting used to having Rivet around. It was sort of how things had happened with Ransom too. Levi hadn't been given a choice about it. Hadn't consciously decided to change his mind about letting anyone into his home or his life, yet after a while, Ransom had become a fixture in both.

If he weren't careful, Rivet would be bolted into them too.

And he couldn't have that. Because he couldn't stand to lose someone he cared about again.

Every day they spent together, it became more difficult than ever to deny that he could have deep feelings for Rivet and Ransom if he allowed himself to be stupid enough to care again.

"Something smells good." She rubbed her growling stomach. Although she wouldn't eat much, Ransom had taken up cooking to tempt her as often and best as he could to ensure she got at least one nutritious meal a day in her. He'd sworn Levi to secrecy about how many times he'd set off the smoke detector or cursed when his concoctions turned out nothing like the recipes he hunted online.

It was adorable, and tugged on Levi's cold, not-quite-dead heart to see the jaded man trying so hard for Rivet, even if she didn't realize it. It was a hell of a lot different than the fast food they'd been surviving on before she'd moved in.

"Nothing fancy. Just a shrimp stir fry I tossed together." Ransom tucked a hand towel in the waistband of his jeans as he poured three portions from his frying pan onto mismatched plates they'd picked up at the thrift shop.

"Damn, what were they feeding you in jail to set your standards so high?" Rivet's genuine laughter did nothing to make Levi less affected by his pair of roommates. "That sounds fancy as fuck to me. Growing up, my idea of gourmet was Chef Boyardee."

Whatever sting she might have unintentionally inflicted by reminding Ransom of his time behind bars, she made up for by crossing to him and slinging her arms around his waist for a quick hug.

"Thanks for doing that." She looked up at Ransom, and the two of them froze.

If this had been any other time or place, Levi was sure they would have been doing a hell of a lot more than staring. Making out or letting dinner get cold while they had dessert first, right there on the kitchen floor.

Rivet shook herself then spun away, bracing her hands on the square kitchen table they made fit by squashing it against one wall, leaving just enough room for all three of them to sit and eat together.

Uh oh. Levi stood even as Ransom sidled up behind her, putting one of his big hands on her shoulder. It squished her oversized black hoodie, making it apparent just how petite she really was compared to the other guy. "You okay?"

Levi joined them, pulling out his stool at the high-top table so that he could hear what she had to say without interrupting.

"You cleaned house today?" she asked barely above a whisper.

Ransom nodded. "I double checked everything myself an hour ago with the spare equipment Jordan gave us. The apartment is clear. You can speak freely."

Rivet sighed and seemed to deflate some. She sank into the seat next to Levi so Ransom set a steaming bowl of pretty damn fine-looking food in front of each of them before taking the stool opposite Levi.

Neither of them said anything, waiting for Rivet to unload in her own time. If she chose to.

She picked up her fork and pushed the caramelized vegetables around without taking a bite before she said, "Sorry, guys. Don't look at me like that. Nothing crazy happened. I'm just having a rough one. It was two years ago today that my gramps died and I went off to track down my mom and started on this road. I just keep putting one foot in front of the other, but when I look back, it seems insane that I've come this far. Would Gramps be pissed that I've spent all this time on a fool's errand?"

Rivet swallowed, then stabbed a shrimp. She blew on it and popped the whole thing in her mouth, groaning in pleasure as the honey ginger sauce thrilled her taste buds. The sound she made was equally as delicious to him, and to Ransom if the tightening of his fingers on his silverware was any indication.

Levi shook himself, concentrating on Rivet's hurt to

distract himself from how desperately he longed to comfort her in much more uncivilized ways.

"I'm sorry." Of course he understood the pain that came with grieving a loved one. Who didn't, really? But some circumstances and losses were harder than others to bear. "He was more like your dad, huh?"

"Yeah." She swallowed hard and stared down into her bowl. Levi hated the desolation in her eyes. "All I ever wanted was for him to be proud of me. If we can knock Angus out..."

"I'm sure he was proud of you regardless," Ransom told her. "Is he the person who taught you how to fix bikes?"

She nodded, the hint of a smile curling her lips. "Mostly I think they needed a babysitter for me sometimes. It was better to give me something to do instead of causing trouble around his shop while he was at work."

"I could see you being a handful as a kid." Levi huffed. She was more than a handful now.

Somehow he adored that about her.

Respected it.

And was pretty damn attracted to it. Their single night together had done absolutely nothing to vent his desire. In fact, the past few weeks had been agony. If he didn't fuck her again soon, which he couldn't, he was going to lose it.

"I'd say that's pretty normal for a girl growing up without her mom and being left to fend for herself too often." Ransom, of course, had the right thing to say. Not that Rivet accepted it.

"How would I know what normal is?" She snorted. "I'm so fucked up *that* seems normal."

119

"It's not like I'm some kind of expert either." Ransom forked some dinner into his mouth and chewed harder than seemed necessary for the tender shrimp and vegetables.

"Hell, my own wife was so horrified by how un-normal I am that she essentially killed herself. I think I take the prize here." Levi wasn't sure his appetite was going to recover after this conversation.

"Shit, guys. I'm sorry." Rivet looked at Ransom and then Levi, her eyes so warm and understanding, he wanted to believe it was possible that he deserved her compassion. "I didn't mean to bring you down too. Especially not after Ransom cooked this awesome meal."

Levi figured for his friend's sake he would have to choke down the rest of his food. And truth be told, after one bite followed another and then another, it warmed him from the inside out, just like their friendship and acceptance.

They ate in silence, each lost in their own thoughts, though he was happy to see that Rivet cleaned her plate. She kicked back and burped loudly, folding her hands over her guts and squeezing as if holding them inside. "Damn, Ransom, that was great. Who the hell taught you how to do that?"

Levi smiled down at his bowl before glancing up in time to see Ransom's sheepish grin. Was that the hint of a fucking blush beneath the guy's neat beard? Holy shit.

He wasn't going to rat out his partner if the guy didn't come clean on his own.

"Uh, the internet?" He winced. "I was trying to impress you."

Levi knew what he really meant was that he was trying

to do what little he could to take care of her. Not out of penance but because he wanted to change too.

"Shit, really?" Rivet seemed appropriately awestruck. "Well, it worked. And...thanks."

Levi wondered if she had any clue about the influence she had over them. In the time they'd spent together, they'd relied on sex to see them through their dark days. Now they actually did this—tried to talk through things and heal each other—rather than simply getting by. "You know, we may not be normal, but hanging out with you is making us better people."

"Me?" Rivet shook her head. "No way. It's you two who are rubbing off on me. I think, for the first time, I'm realizing I want more than simply to make Angus pay. I've started wondering what life might be like after all of this is over and whether I could really go back to an ordinary grind at Hot Rides, with my sister and my niece."

"You can. You *should*." Levi wanted to tell her to take off right then, but he knew she wouldn't appreciate that suggestion, so he bit his tongue.

Ransom put down his fork and squeezed her hand. "Why don't we pretend that all three of us can do that someday? Let's spend tonight doing what's normal for us."

"You mean wash the dishes then kick your ass at video games?" Rivet perked up at that.

Ransom's rumbling laughter was every bit as nourishing to Levi as the food he'd prepared. "Yeah, that."

Sounded like a good idea to Levi, too. He scooped his and Ransom's plates into his hands, and let Rivet take their glasses and silverware. He washed, she dried, and Ransom looked on their domestic activities with a satisfied smirk that made Levi wish they were going to entertain themselves in a far more basic fashion.

Instead, a little while later, Rivet bounced onto the couch next to him, settling into her favorite position with her legs crossed. Even still, she didn't take up more than her third of the sofa. She claimed her controller and held it over her stacked ankles, ready to go.

Levi loaded up a first-person shooter and got lost in the cathartic act of blowing away their enemies. The three of them worked together as a hell of a team, clearing level after level of the game where they assumed the role of heroes fighting against mobsters intent on destroying law and order.

They probably should have opted for something less realistic.

Because as he watched the final boss of the area creep around the corner and put his gun right in Rivet's character's face, he began to struggle to draw in a breath. Hyperventilating, he was worthless to assist. Victim to his own panic, he was swiftly eliminated by a threat he hadn't even seen coming.

Rivet roared and, on instinct, shot the assailant who'd taken him out several times despite the fact that it was too late.

Ransom jerked beside her as if he was reliving his past and his own reflexive actions in defense of a loved one. Hell, maybe he was. He stood there in the game, completely frozen, and someone assassinated him from behind.

Levi watched the realistic avatar drop to the ground.

Rivet shrieked and ran to him, crouching over his lifeless body. Distracted, she didn't notice as the boss circled around and came up behind her. Before Levi could even call out a warning to her, she took a bullet to the back of her head. In graphic detail, pixelated brains, blood, and gore splattered across the screen.

Levi thought he might be sick. He stared, unblinking, as Rivet's corpse piled on top of Ransom's.

He bolted to his feet.

No, not again. He couldn't do that again.

His controller clattered to the plank flooring.

"Son of a bitch!" Rivet glared at the screen, pissed that they'd completely fallen apart. "Let's try it again."

"I can't." Levi's hands went numb. His heart was about to explode out of his chest. A ringing started in his ears, drowning out Ransom as he asked Levi...something.

Rivet stood and put her hands out toward him, slowly, carefully, as if he was a wild animal.

Hell, maybe he was.

What the fuck were they doing? Risking her life along with theirs? He should have forced her to stay behind in Middletown. Fuck it if that made them weaker or less likely to succeed. Nothing was worth gambling her life. Or Ransom's.

"Rivet. I think you should go." Levi locked stares with her. "Please. Take your bike, right now. You can make it to Middletown before dawn. Jordan can keep you locked up in Kason's lodge until this is over. Please leave."

"You're sending me away? Just like my mom?" Though her head barely cleared his shoulders, she was still imposing as she turned bright red. "Fuck you! What right do you have? Just because I told you I was having doubts for a second... I'm not weak. I can handle myself and I *will* see this through."

"It's not because of what you said before." He wished he could wrap her in a bear hug, but even touching her that much with the blood still oozing across the TV was too much.

"Then why? Because I let you fuck me?" She shoved him. "You're right, that was a mistake too."

Levi staggered away from her and Ransom then. He kept going with the momentum, heading for the door. When he tripped over his boots, he decided he needed some air, so he jammed his feet into them, then snagged his helmet.

"Where are you going?" Ransom called.

"For a ride." It was the only thing besides fucking that would clear his head so he could think straight. Like this, he wasn't any good to any of them.

Like this, he would doom them all to the exact scenario that had played out in excruciating detail in their living room.

"Want me to come with you?" Ransom asked looking back and forth between him and Rivet, who shook with rage.

"No. Stay with her. She needs you."

"I don't need anyone." Rivet argued, her head held high and her chin tilted defiantly, making Levi hard in an instant.

"We can keep telling ourselves that, but unfortunately it doesn't make it true." Levi sighed. He was terrified, running scared, because he realized it was already too late.

If something happened to Rivet or Ransom on this mission, he would never recover. It was like he'd jumped out of a plane and was now praying his parachute would open. Otherwise, he was already doomed.

Either way, the die had been cast and he was just waiting to see what they'd rolled.

Yeah, he definitely needed to ride.

"Don't go too far," Ransom reminded him. "Stay in Wildfire territory unless you want to be a trophy for one of Angus's enemies."

Levi nodded curtly. He didn't give a shit about his own life anymore, but if he got himself injured or worse, he would only make things harder for Ransom and Rivet.

And that he couldn't stand.

"I'll be back. Just need some space." He put his helmet on and slammed down the visor before running from the home they were making together and the life he would lose, either way, once this assignment was finished.

13

Ransom didn't give a fuck if he shouldn't. He crossed the room to Rivet and crushed her in his arms. "He doesn't mean to hurt you."

"Us. And so what if it comes natural or he's doing it on purpose? The end result is the same." She surprised him by yielding, tucking her face against his chest and holding on to him as if she needed someone to cling to in the turbulence of their life, even if she didn't often let on to that fact.

Of course, she'd already admitted she was struggling that day. And Levi had stomped on her again when he'd freaked out too. They were a hot mess. All of them. Ransom included.

But damn if he didn't feel ten feet tall when he stood there and rocked her gently until her ragged breathing slowed, like for once he was actually doing what he'd always tried to do most, look after those who were important to him and keep them safe. Support them so they could be happy and whole.

He rubbed her back and leaned his cheek against the top of her head. It was the best he could do to shelter her from whatever was coming for them as well as the ghosts of their past. Torn, he wished like Levi that he could whisk her away from it all, out of danger.

"Maybe he isn't entirely wrong, though." Ransom tentatively prodded at the crack Levi had opened in Rivet's objections. "If you're having doubts, or struggling with staying, there isn't any shame in tapping out."

"If you know how his suggestion cut me, and you see how what he's doing is selfish, then you're not about to pull the same shit, are you?" Rivet shoved away enough that she could level some serious side eye at him.

Given that she was so close and his legs were spread to brace them both against the onslaught of emotions running wild through them, his balls were in the danger zone. So he chose his words carefully. "No. I'm not going to try to force you to leave, but I can't lie either. I'd be much happier if you, or Levi, or both of you were out of danger."

"What about you?" She raised a brow at him, making him wish he could kiss her until she let him off the hook and they found much more pleasurable ways to hash things out between them.

"My life is worthless anyway, Rivet." He dropped his arms and shrugged because it was simply the truth. "It was over the day I ended someone else's."

"I don't believe that." She shook her head. "You're here, fighting for something, same as Levi and I are. There has to be a chance, even if it's a tiny one, we can make up for the shit we did or we wouldn't be bothering, would we?"

"What do you mean?" Ransom hesitated, feeling like he was being set up.

"Tell me more about what you said that night in the hotel." Rivet bit her lip as she peeked up at him, her ire replaced with curiosity. "I want to know exactly why you were in prison."

"No, you don't. You won't be able to look at me the same way after." If he could have curled up into himself then, he would have. He hated to remember the person he'd been back then and the chain of events that had led him into the blackest moments of his life.

He would much rather her think of him as the guy who'd learned to cook so what little she allowed herself to eat was decent.

Rivet wasn't about to back down, though—it was one of the things he admired most about her.

She put her hands on his chest, practically branding him with her splayed fingers when she leaned into him, putting her full weight on her straight-locked arms.

He could have resisted her, but he honestly didn't feel like it.

He was tired, and lonely, and...weak. As always.

Wasn't that exactly what he was trying to tell her? He wasn't half as good as Levi.

So he went where she directed him, sinking down onto their frumpy sofa when she pushed on his shoulders. Nothing could have shocked him more than when she followed him, climbing onto the dipped cushions, her knees bracketing his thighs.

Without thinking, he looped his arms around her waist, his hands meeting in the small of her back. Hey, at least he barely managed to keep from sliding them lower to grab her ass.

It had been forever since he'd held a woman. BP, before prison, he hadn't valued his partners and what he'd shared with them. A player, he'd loved and left so many women he'd had no idea how lucky he was to have them, if only for a night. Since being locked up, he'd learned to adapt, at first closing his eyes and imagining a lady when he'd let someone blow him. Over time, he'd accepted that he enjoyed sex with men even if he hadn't realized the possibility or given himself permission to explore before fate had given him the perfect excuse. He especially enjoyed unleashing the rougher side of his sexuality, which he'd always felt guilty about doing when he slept with women. That didn't mean he didn't prefer the ladies—except for Levi, of course. But Levi was the only person he'd ever gotten naked with whom he gave a shit about.

And that only proved what slime he was. For using people to get off when he didn't care about more than giving them an orgasm or two in return. He deserved to go down with Angus and Wildfire. Maybe from the ashes, he could be reborn, become a person who did the right thing instead of only wishing he did.

"Tell me," Rivet murmured, her lips close enough that he could taste them if he leaned forward even a fraction of an inch. "I came clean to you."

"You want the truth? Here's the fucking truth..." Ransom stared directly into her warm eyes as he said, "When the shit starts to rain down on us all, I'm going to be the one to take the brunt of it. Because my life was over the night I ended someone else's. And until I give mine in return, justice won't truly be served."

"Hey. Don't talk like that." Rivet's chest rose and fell rapidly. Her eyes flicked around the room. Hell, he'd never seen her truly scared before, though he should have plenty of times by then.

"Why not? It's true." He shrugged. "My little sister came to me and told me some dude had stolen the purse I gave her for Christmas. What I didn't realize, because I was off working any jobs I could get—including some shady shit like hotwiring cars that had earned me a couple priors and kept the judge and jury from being too sympathetic to my dumb ass—to keep us afloat and chasing ass in between instead of paying as much attention to her as I should have been, is that the thing was crammed full of drugs. She was only seventeen and had been dealing. I hear she was pretty good at it too, until she tried to double-cross her boss. He'd let her off easy, reclaimed his stash and told her to get lost, maybe because he actually gave a shit about her. And when I busted into his house to get it back, he didn't take kindly to me crashing in. He pulled a gun, and so did I. Hell, I'd never even used one before, but I was outraged over what I thought was no more than a couple hundred bucks for a designer bag from an outlet store and what little my sister would have had in her wallet. Stupid. I probably should have wondered why she was so fired up that she insisted on coming with me, instead of trying to talk me out of my idiotic plan. But when that asshole drew and aimed at her instead of me, I lost it. I fired first and asked questions later."

Unfortunately, it was too late to bring the guy back by then.

"I killed someone over something meaningless. I didn't mean to, didn't think it would come to that, didn't realize there was so much more in play, couldn't let my sister die as a result of my idiotic choice to smash that door down, and the asshole certainly wasn't some kind of innocent, but it happened just the same." Ransom's head fell back against the couch cushion. He couldn't even find the strength to hold it up anymore, the weight of what he'd done crashing down on him all over again. "Lost my sister over it all too. She never came to any of my court dates or visited me in prison. Not once. What happened that day destroyed everything."

"How old were you?" Rivet wondered as she settled lower, sitting fully in his lap as she laid her head on his shoulder.

How could she even stand to touch him now that she knew the truth?

Even his own sister had left him to rot after what he'd done. Why would Rivet stick by him?

He wasn't sure, but he hung onto her because he needed something to keep him grounded. "Nineteen."

"You were young. Immature. Same as me." She sighed. "Back then, I thought things were a lot simpler than they are. Now I know better. You can't always fix problems as easily and directly as you would like."

"No kidding. And the consequences of learning that lesson can be steep. You and Levi know that as well as I do. And that's why we're terrified. Both of us. For you and each other." He tipped his head forward so he could look into her eyes. The remorse he saw in hers mirrored his own. In that instant, his heart found a match. She could truly understand him, even if she couldn't repair him any more than she could herself. Neither did she label him junk for his dings and dents.

"Wow. We're really screwed up, aren't we?" Rivet shook her head ruefully.

"Pretty much." As if to prove it, he made another

colossal mistake. Because it would have been impossible to ignore the impulses that encouraged him to console her.

His fingers tightened on her hips. Bony though they were at the moment, he could feel how lush they could become if she let them. He wished he could feed her, nourish her body and mind and shattered soul. If he could put her back together maybe that would count for something. Maybe that would go a little way toward making up for the sins he'd committed.

Or maybe he was trying to justify kissing her.

Because that's what he did.

Ransom held her close to him as he lowered his head and nudged her mouth with his. Instead of fighting him, she bent too, meeting him halfway.

She sighed, buffeting him with a puff of her breath before taking his lower lip between hers. The rake of her teeth on the sensitive area only turned him on more. Rivet wasn't easily broken. She could handle him, and Levi. If things had been different...

Well, then none of them would have met because she would be happy, and Levi would be whole, and he would be locked up.

He hesitated, but she refused to let him retreat. Not after he'd initiated the contact. Instead she cajoled him out of his foul mood with low hums and the light pressure of her mouth sucking on his lip. And when he realized that he was taking more than he was giving, he vowed to quit being so damn selfish.

He growled and clasped Rivet's hips, drawing her tighter to him as he kissed her back, more ferociously this time. He might not have fucked her that night in the hotel, but he was sure as hell going to make up for it right then.

The sounds she made as he skipped sipping from her lips in favor of plundering them only encouraged him to do it more. She matched him kiss for kiss, swiping her tongue into his mouth so that he could suck on it.

At that point, he lost all awareness of their surroundings. The voices shouting reasons why this was a terrible idea were drowned out by a rush of pleasure and anticipation more powerful than the drugs his sister had sold to junkies like Levi's wife.

Just like before, he acted on instinct and emotion instead of rationality.

He was fucked.

And apparently so was Rivet.

Or they would be soon. Because her hands were roaming now, covering the expanse of his chest and the bulging muscles of his arms, before sinking lower, toward his raging erection.

Ransom groaned in between kisses, "Sevan."

She snapped to attention at that, her entire body going stiff. It was reckless to use her real name here, or ever for that matter. But he needed her to know that this wasn't about who they were pretending to be, but the people they were deep inside.

Too bad she didn't know his real name to return the favor.

Rivet sat there, blinking up at him, as if trying to decide whether to put the brakes on or to hit the gas. Fortunately, they were saved from any more blunders when boot steps clomped up the stairs to their apartment.

Rivet sprang from the couch and her place in Ransom's arms. Her flushed face, spiky hair in disarray, and wild eyes made it obvious what they'd been up to. At least it would be apparent to Levi, who opened the door and stood there, his stare ping-ponging between them.

When his gaze dipped for a moment, to the bulge in Ransom's pants, Ransom knew they were utterly busted.

"Shit. Want me to actually go for that ride?" He slammed his eyes closed, then turned as if to go. "Didn't mean to interrupt."

Funny that he didn't remind them how stupid they were being fooling around in the first place.

"No, don't go," Rivet begged as Ransom said, "Stay."

And he hoped Levi understood what he meant. Not stay because they were going to come to their senses and keep their hands off each other. No, he meant stay because he wanted to share this feeling with Levi, who adored Rivet every bit as much as he did.

Levi rested his forehead on the doorjamb, one foot in their apartment and one outside. Yet he didn't take another step, didn't close the door on them, leaving himself out in the cold darkness. He said, "I should leave, but I can't."

"Same goes," Rivet replied, and that was all it took.

Levi whipped around, shutting the door and keeping himself there, with them. He said, "I'm sorry. I shouldn't even have suggested it. I'm just freaking out because...I care about you. It will kill me if anything happens to you. Either of you."

He charged Rivet and scooped her into his arms. She wrapped her legs around Levi and hung on as he slid his hands up her back, pressing her close to his heart.

"If we stick together, we're going to be okay." Rivet kissed Levi then, making Ransom's dick throb as he watched the two most attractive people he'd ever met go at each other. He could watch them forever.

Or at least he could have, if something hadn't interrupted the moment.

Something stirred in his pants.

He rubbed his dick as he rose, coming up behind Rivet so that she was surrounded by their heat and muscles. Hopefully she understood they would protect her as best they could. He wrapped his arms not only around her, but Levi as well.

Except the buzzing in his pants returned. And this time he realized it wasn't his body quaking in response to Rivet's kisses or Levi's molten stare. Damn it! It was his cell phone in his pocket.

The only people who had the number were Angus and the Wildfire garage. *Shit!*

He ripped himself from Levi's embrace and stumbled backward. The doubt and hurt written in his expression made Ransom wish he could reach out and reassure his partner that he wanted to continue what they'd been doing as much as Levi did. But they couldn't.

He jammed his hand in his pocket and withdrew his phone, wiggling it back and forth quickly so Rivet and Levi realized he was getting a call and wouldn't say anything incriminating when he answered. "Hey."

"What the fuck took so long?" Angus asked, his question sharp.

"Was taking a piss." Hopefully that explained his panting. As if he'd had to dash for his ringing phone in another room instead of trying to recover from having his breath stolen by the emotions squeezing everything else out of his chest.

"Next time piss on your boots and answer the fucking phone when I call you," Angus snarled. "Get in here for an emergency club meeting. I'm going to let our new

136

sergeant-at-arms take out my frustration on the last people here. Don't let it be you."

"I'll be right there, pres." Ransom grimaced and Levi ran his hand through his hair. Then he jabbed his finger at his chest before pointing at the phone. He wanted to come along. Rivet nodded vigorously too.

Damn it. He couldn't deny he felt better about going in with some backup. Even if it meant putting them in danger. And that was fucked up. Everything he had sworn not to do.

Still, he said, "You want my roomies too?"

Angus hesitated only for a moment before he said, "Yes. All members. Just hurry the fuck up. Use that bike of yours for something more than showing off for once."

"Got it. Be there pronto."

"Good." Angus hung up.

"You know, he could really use some better phone manners." Ransom tried to lighten the mood when they all knew this was it, what they'd been waiting for. If Angus was this fired up, something was going down.

"I'm going to wear the camera Jordan gave us," Ransom told them.

It wasn't up for debate. They might be coming along for the ride, but he was going to take the most risk. This could be it. They had a chance to get more dirt. He only hoped it was what they needed to bring Angus down for good.

Slowly, Levi nodded. Rivet slammed her eyes closed, then took a deep breath.

When she opened them, they were clear and hard. Nothing like when she'd been kissing him. She nodded. "Let's do this."

Each of them concentrated on preparing themselves

in the limited time they had. It wasn't until they were riding side by side by side toward Wildfire that Ransom realized there was no turning back now. Not on their mission and not on the relationship that was developing between them despite their best attempts to squash it. They were fucked.

14

"**S**on of a bitch. These guys are the biggest cock blockers of all time," Rivet grumbled to herself as they climbed onto their motorcycles. Instead of whatever had been about to happen upstairs, she prepared to deal with Angus. Not to mention whatever emergency had spurred him to demand everyone leave their families and whatever fun times they might have been about to enjoy for more club business.

Hadn't they had enough for one fucking day? What could be so important that it couldn't wait until morning? At least they had a few minutes of speeding through the crisp night air, the petrichor left behind by an earlier rain shower reminding her of the impending spring. Things wouldn't be dead and cold forever. They would blossom again.

Could she say the same for her, Ransom, and Levi?

She'd been about to find out, but now she'd have to wait. She hated Angus more than ever.

Rivet dreaded being summoned to Wildfire at any time, but especially at night it seemed even more evil than she knew it was. The black building glowed eerily in the stillness after midnight, never left completely dark to prevent their enemies from sneaking up undetected. They rolled into the lot as fog swirled above the pavement.

Nothing good ever came of one of these late-night—or early-morning, she should say—meetings. Shit was about to get real.

In some sick way, she was glad. Because every time something like this happened, it might be the exact missing piece they needed to complete the puzzle they were trying to construct. The one that would end this madness once and for all. If they were incredibly lucky.

If some small part of herself regretted that it would mean her time living with Ransom and Levi was over, well, that was pure selfish insanity. So she smothered that foolishness as she followed them inside, trying her best not to check out their asses encased in well-worn denim beneath the hem of their cuts. That was the only thing she didn't like about how they looked, and she knew they wished they could rip them off as much as she did.

As they came inside, Angus was barking orders. "Put the old ladies in the lounge. We have business."

Red did as he was told, ushering the women—some high or drunk off their barely covered asses—into the adjoining space. How the fuck late did these guys stay here and party every night? No wonder they were no help with early-morning appointments at the garage.

A massive reinforced barn door was rolled across the wide doorway until it slammed shut against the far side of the doorway, and locked, trapping the one-percenters in the heart of the Wildfire clubhouse. Angus perched on a black, tufted-leather wingback chair which sat on a dais, making it clear who was in charge, just in case anyone forgot or developed any mutinous ideas.

Red and Stix sat across from Ransom, Levi, and Rivet, who occupied a couch by themselves, shooting them nervous glances. Everyone knew the stakes were getting higher and higher. And that Angus would stop at nothing to grow his empire, maybe beyond what was wise.

Rivet risked looking at Wildfire's president. She couldn't get over how different he looked from Walker, despite the physical similarities to his son. No welcoming smile or laugh lines around his eyes or the hint of good humor that underlay Walker's own brand of fierceness.

It was like Angus had lost every bit of humanity he'd once possessed, his eyes so dark they reminded her of a crow's. Soulless.

"What's up, pres?" Red asked as if the anticipation was killing him. Hell, maybe it was.

A few guys murmured as they gathered around the center of the room. The rest, another two dozen or so, were smart enough to be quiet and wait to be informed of whatever had riled Angus.

They would be expected to carry out whatever scheme he was cooking up that had been important enough to call an immediate meeting to address. He certainly wasn't about to announce a club Secret Santa exchange or next month's potluck theme.

"Those piece of shit Savage Skulls have apparently forgotten their place. Maybe they're bad at geography. I've been hearing rumors that they're dealing drugs and running guns, encroaching on our territory. Worse, our customers have started complaining that their shit is better than ours. Last week alone, there were reports of five overdoses in our territory. People thinking they were getting our stuff, but scoring Savage Skulls' and whatever else they're adding to it instead. We don't need that kind of attention on us."

Rivet's hackles went up as Levi fidgeted beside her. Most anyone else probably wouldn't notice the subtle difference in his posture, but to her it was as obvious as white smoke pouring out of an engine that was about to seize. Ransom cleared his throat. He could feel it too, and though he couldn't say anything, he was warning Levi to keep calm the only way he was able.

"So I got my hands on some of it, to see if these assholes are telling the truth. Who wants some free shit?" Angus grinned as he unfurled his fingers and revealed a baggie of white powder resting on his palm. "Test it out for me so we can verify this bullshit."

The club members might have been outlaws, thugs, and worse. But they weren't that stupid. No one volunteered to be Angus's guinea pig.

"I guess our newest member should do it." Angus swung his head to grin at Rivet. "Time to prove yourself like you wanted to so bad, kid."

Levi's thigh tensed along hers, turning into something that resembled a timber more than flesh and bone.

Oh fuck. Drugs weren't her thing. She'd never tried them, not wanting to be out of control or—god forbid—end up liking them too much. Besides, she'd never had that much cash to blow on getting high instead of feeding herself or her family.

Surprisingly, it was Stix who came to her rescue. "Why waste that stuff on him when one of the old ladies would get a kick out of it?"

"You know..." Angus stood then and strode behind

Stix, making the man tense up. "You're pretty fucking smart sometimes."

He clapped his hand on Stix's shoulder, making the man bounce in his seat. Then marched over to the barn door and opened it just enough to call to the club whores, half of whom had been chained to Wildfire by their addictions in the first place.

"I've got something special for whoever wants to blow me later." Angus grinned while he waggled the baggie of drugs as if he was offering a dog a bone.

He'd barely finished making his offer before one of the women leapt forward, her boobs nearly spilling out of her slashed shirt as she dove for the stash, elbowing another woman out of the way for the opportunity—both for a complimentary high and to gain status in the club by pleasing Angus. "I'll do it."

"Good girl." He winked at her. "When you're finished, I'll thank you properly."

She smiled shyly up at him as if he'd granted her a massive award in addition to her free drugs. Angus slung his arm around her shoulder and dragged her inside, slamming the door shut and locking it once more. He led the woman into the center of the assembled gang and shoved her down onto the thin blood-red rug covering the concrete there.

"I take it you've got what you need in your purse?" He lifted a brow at her.

"I'm always prepared." She smiled in a way she probably thought was seductive, though Rivet had to look away as the woman retrieved her paraphernalia. "What is this?" she asked.

"That's what you're going to tell me," Angus informed her. "Hurry up."

It wasn't long before Rivet caught the flash of a lighter in the corner of her eye. When she flicked her gaze back to the woman, she had something tied around her bicep and was using what definitely did not appear to be a clean needle to suck fluid out of bent spoon.

Fuck, were they really going to sit there and watch this woman shoot up some mystery substance? Sure, drugs were rampant in the club and the old ladies who hung around were no strangers to them, but still. That wasn't some kind of human experimentation.

Levi's fingers were clenched so hard on his knee they were turning blue at the knuckles.

Rivet had never wanted something as badly in her life than to cover his hand with hers and reassure him, but she couldn't do that. Not without getting killed. And also because she was not confident in the slightest that this was going to end well for any of them. Especially the woman shooting that shit into her veins.

Immediately, the woman sighed, then closed her eyes to wait for the effects to kick in. Watching her made Rivet aware of what odds Levi had been fighting to save his wife. He couldn't blame himself for being unable to help her recover from a sickness as terminal as this. But he did.

He coughed as if he was choking on his own tongue when, in less than a minute, the woman started to laugh. She shouted, "Whatever that was, it's some gooooooooooood shit!"

Unfortunately, her celebration was short lived.

In another minute, she'd begun to lose the flush from her cheeks, her skin going gray as if the life leeched right out of it as Rivet watched.

Oh no. No, no.

The next thing she noticed was how the woman's

pupils contracted until they were barely pinpoints. But she didn't get truly concerned until the woman slumped, her breathing growing shallow, interspersed with ominous gurgles that had never been made by a healthy human being.

"Guess that answers that," Angus said with a shrug. Then he got angry, his rage over being duped rather than the life he was about to steal. He kicked a lamp, sending it crashing to the ground. The woman didn't even flinch. "I'm going to kill every last one of those Savage Skulls."

Not before he murdered this poor woman right in front of her, Ransom, Levi, and the rest of the gang.

Levi...who was vibrating with frantic energy that had no outlet.

Rivet looked between Ransom and the rest of the guys in the room. Red and Stix were staring at their boots as if unable to even glance at the woman beginning to gasp for every last molecule of air she could draw into her lungs.

It was even worse once she went quiet and absolutely still. Entirely limp as she flopped to her back on the ground. From a few feet away, Rivet could see the tips of her fingers turning purple beneath nails chewed to the quick.

"She's not breathing!" Levi shouted from beside her.

Rivet was terrified. Not only for the woman losing the fight to live right in front of them, but for Levi. Could he endure this? Would he break and give them away? If he survived, would he ever be whole again? He was already struggling, wrestling with the demons inside him. She feared this would only make them stronger.

He broke from the couch, tore across the room, and dove over the bar, sliding across it on his flank like he was a goddamned stunt double for *The Dukes of Hazzard*. He rummaged around beneath the counter for a moment before returning with a metal tackle box Rivet recognized as their version of a first aid kit from the time one of the mechanics had damn near sliced his finger off with an angle grinder.

Levi flung open the lid as Ransom and Rivet dashed toward the woman who appeared lifeless. In less time than it took for Rivet to prop her up and feel for a pulse, which was there but faint, Levi had returned to their sides. He unwrapped a sterile needle from its package and plunged it into a vial before turning both upside down.

He drew some of the fluid into the needle, then held it between his teeth as he and Ransom rolled the woman onto her stomach. Without hesitating, he yanked her dress up then stabbed her deep in the upper, outer quadrant of her ass and depressed the plunger.

When he turned her back over, he began to breathe for her.

Rivet and Ransom stood back and let him do his thing. He was so sure and steady in his motions as he worked relentlessly to save the woman's life. For two to three minutes, which seemed at least a year long each, he gave her CPR. The entire time, no one said a word. And when Levi's patient gasped and groaned, then rolled to her side and was sick, Rivet had never been so relieved.

Levi fell backward, plopping onto his ass as Ransom held the woman's hair back and promised her she was going to be okay. Rivet thought that might have been an overstatement, but at least she wouldn't be dead.

Holy fucking shit! That had been close.

If her heart was pounding in her chest, Levi's had to be damn near wrecked.

But she couldn't hug him, or console him, or tell him

how fucking proud she was of him. Not with all the witnesses staring at them in shock. If they'd blown their cover, then so be it. They'd deal with the consequences together.

So she got to her feet with a sneer of disgust—inspired by Wildfire and its leader, not the woman who was clearly suffering and needed help—and went back to the couch as if she was as heartless as Angus or as cowardly as the rest of the men who followed him blindly and hadn't lifted a single finger to help.

Shortly, Levi and Ransom joined her, leaving the woman to recover on her own. She started complaining of a headache and begged to use again as the Narcan put her into instant withdrawal. No one was going to let her do that, though. If only because those drugs were valuable, and to them, she was not. Besides, bodies were a liability and a pain to get rid of.

Levi sat there, his elbows on his knees, his face in his hands as he struggled to draw in a single deep breath. Angus approached, his boots landing directly in front of Levi's.

"Where'd you learn to do that?" he asked, his head cocked as if he was sort of disappointed the woman was still with them.

Levi looked up then and let Angus see the torment swirling in his gorgeous blue eyes.

"My ex-wife was a junkie." True enough, Rivet knew. But she'd bet her bike that he'd learned how to reverse an overdose during his training as a first responder when in the police academy.

"Is that why you left her and why you won't touch the old ladies now?" Angus wondered. "I've always assumed you considered yourself too good for some easy ass."

Levi's self-loathing was genuine when he replied, "More like I'm not good enough for anyone. There wasn't anybody sober enough to jab Laurel when she overdosed. So yeah, I'm not really into women who like this shit anymore."

Angus nodded. "Hmm. Interesting. It ain't easy to lose your old lady. Fucks a man up, doesn't it?"

For one moment, Rivet wondered if he really could identify with Levi's pain. Even though he'd been responsible for ending her mother's life, she thought...just maybe...he might have loved her. Maybe the final splinter of his humanity had died along with her. Unlike Levi, he *had* been responsible for that and he deserved to pay for it too. He would if she had to die seeing to it.

Fucking bastard.

"What are you going to do about this?" Ransom asked, nudging Angus in the direction they needed him to go.

Angus snarled, his ire returning in a flash as if it had never receded. "I'm going to teach those bastard Savage Skulls a lesson. This is war. Either they're going to give the business to us or they're going to pay us for the right to trade in our territory like they should have been doing all along. And since they seem to have forgotten how things work, they can give us an extra cut as interest on what they've passed through already."

Holy. Fucking. Shit.

There it was. Rivet forced herself to keep breathing. That statement was hardcore proof of racketeering. Everything Jordan needed to bust Angus on RICO charges, if the president went through with his threat.

Levi nodded as if he agreed with that course of action. "We fight. When?"

"Three nights from tonight. We're going to need every

member there to get through their men so I can have the conversation I need, president to president." Angus glanced at them, then smirked. "Even you, Rivet. It's time you showed me what you're really made of, don't you think?"

Nope. Nope, she did not think that was a good idea.

Still she smiled as if she'd waited her whole life for this chance to prove herself to him. Hopefully she'd be smiling even wider when they carted him off in handcuffs. "I can't wait."

"You will. Three days." He glared as if she would be crazy enough to go rogue, again, and infiltrate the Savage Skulls on her own. "We need all the weapons we can gather, and all the men too."

He handed out orders, mobilizing the club in one of the biggest operations she'd witnessed since joining Wildfire. At least she was a full member now, not a prospect, and had direct access to the action. When the meeting had adjourned and Rivet had made sure the old lady who'd nearly fucking died had been placed in the care of her friends, they followed the rest of the members outside as they began to disperse.

The roar of engines at least soothed her as she climbed onto her motorcycle beside Levi and Ransom. Levi hadn't said a fucking word. Not a peep. He stared straight ahead like a zombie as he started his bike and waited for Ransom to lead them home.

Rivet couldn't get to their apartment soon enough. It wasn't much, but at least it wasn't here. And if they were together, they would be safe. Levi was going to need some time to decompress. They had to get him out of there before he crumbled or lashed out and tried to wring Angus's neck with his bare hands.

Ransom must have been able to feel it too. He barked, "Levi, let's go. We have shit to do."

Yeah, like calling Jordan to tell him what was about to go down and how close they were to finally achieving their goal. If they could stay alive, and sane, that long.

15

Levi stood behind Ransom and Rivet, who were huddled around their kitchen table, debriefing Jordan via a secure videoconference. Hearing Ransom relate the deep shit they were about to step into in such a matter of fact fashion didn't make him like it any better.

He paced their tiny kitchen. The floorboards squeaked with every circuit.

"Guys, I'm sure you're aware, but...this is risky as fuck." Jordan frowned. "I agree that along with the recording you just transferred to our file locker, which will show premeditation, if you can get footage of the attack and/or payoff in the form of contraband to stave one off that would give us everything we need to nail him with racketeering."

"Which is why I can't fucking wait." Rivet cracked her knuckles.

The sound of her joints popping set Levi on edge. Okay, fine, he'd been on edge since he'd watched her avatar hit the ground on their TV earlier, but his case of the nerves had grown until it was pretty much a full-blown panic attack given what had happened at the clubhouse.

Rivet leaned in toward the screen even as Levi wished he could shove her through the secure connection to Jordan as easily as they transferred data. Ransom droned on like a robot in the background, relaying every piece of information he could for the record. Levi couldn't focus on what he was saying.

He shifted his gaze to Rivet, her elbows planted on the table as she nodded along with Ransom's report, every bit as committed as she'd always been to their mission.

It was him who was changing. Him who was cracking. And if they relied on him and he didn't have his shit together...

The vision of her and Ransom's lifeless bodies, dripping fresh blood, exploded in his memory. Instead of the cartoon version, he imagined it was real.

It was all too easy to picture.

His stomach lurched.

Levi rushed to the bathroom in case he was sick. He stood there, gripping the edges of their porcelain pedestal sink, staring at himself in the mirror. Who the fuck was this man staring back at him?

He hardly recognized the hard angles of his cheekbones and jaw or the dark shadows under his eyes. His face was covered in scruff and he felt...dirty. Filthy.

So he rotated, flicking on the shower as hot as it would go before quickly ridding himself of his socks, jeans, briefs, and long-sleeved shirt. Then he climbed into the old-fashioned boxy tub, drawing the curtain behind him.

Was he losing it? Yup, sure seemed so.

How was he going to last through one of the most

important assignments of his career—hell, his life—when he was already falling apart? He'd never been more scared, not even when he'd practiced coming out to his wife about being bisexual, and look how that had gone.

Levi stood under the scalding spray, wishing it would do something to wipe clean his conscience and his soul.

Ah, fuck.

He braced his hands on the shower wall and let his forehead rest on the tiles to keep him steady. His breathing grew ragged and he was glad the spray from the shower kept him from telling for sure if he was crying like a baby as he broke down. His ragged inhalation drew droplets of water along with it into his lungs and he began to cough as if he was drowning.

Hell, maybe he was. He had to get it together.

If Rivet or Ransom saw him like this, it would add to their own worries and misgivings, putting them in greater danger than they already were. He pounded on the tile surround.

"Hey." Ransom's soft voice startled him, freezing him in place.

Levi didn't dare turn around or the other man would be able to read everything—his doubts, his fears, and his regrets—on his face. When he didn't react, Ransom shocked him again by pushing aside the shower curtain and climbing in behind him. When he wrapped his arms around Levi and crushed Levi's back to his chest, it was clear Ransom hadn't even bothered to take off his jeans or T-shirt.

This wasn't wise.

It also wasn't possible to tell him to leave when Levi needed the false security of his embrace so desperately right then. He lifted his hands to Ransom's forearms, which banded around his chest, and clung to them as if the other man's flesh was the only thing stopping Levi from circling the drain before he slipped into the sewer with the rest of his filth.

"You're okay. I've got you," Ransom murmured in his ear. Whether that was so Rivet didn't realize Levi was having a mental breakdown or because they hadn't swept this room for bugs since they'd returned, he wasn't sure.

"Not okay," he rasped through gritted teeth as he shivered in Ransom's hold, despite the steamy water pouring over them both, plastering them together.

"Look at me." Ransom manhandled Levi, turning him around so they could stare into each other's eyes. "You were not responsible for what happened—either today, or years ago. You're doing the best you can. We can't save them all. Tonight you did a hell of a job, though."

Levi would like to agree, but he couldn't. Despite the proximity of Ransom and his warm brown eyes, all he could see was the vacant stare of the woman who'd been willing to sacrifice herself for Angus's peace of mind. Or the similar one Laurel had leveled at him when he'd discovered her body outside an abandoned warehouse used by local druggies, left behind by people afraid to be caught under the influence.

Ransom gripped his shoulders then and shook him, hard. "Levi. Come on."

When he couldn't snap out of it, Ransom groaned, then leaned in. He crashed their mouths together as if he was performing CPR, attempting to kiss some life back into Levi.

It might have worked, too.

The adrenaline and terror swamping him fueled his reaction, amplifying the natural attraction he had for his partner. Making out with Ransom helped him feel safe and desired and, in some weird way, normal despite the fact that their relationship was anything but that.

As Ransom's handler, they should never have crossed this line, and he certainly shouldn't have been so willing to give the other man ultimate control, but both of them were rule breakers. So he didn't fight, and chased the only spark of goodness and light he could find in the darkness that had become his existence.

Levi fisted Ransom's sopping shirt and hung on to him, giving himself over to the twisted beauty of their fierce exchange. He needed a break, if only for a few minutes, from the horror surrounding them.

As incredible as Ransom's kisses were, that alone wasn't going to cut it.

He reached down and unfastened Ransom's pants. It was dangerous without sweeping the room, but he didn't care right then. "More. Need more. Something stronger to get all this shit out of my head. Please."

Ransom grunted. He seemed unsure. If he pushed Levi away now, he would go insane. So he dropped to his knees and finished baring the other man, tugging his jeans a few inches down his massive thighs to reveal his semi-erect cock and balls. Good thing he didn't believe in underwear.

Levi did his best to eradicate Ransom's doubts by taking his partner's shaft in his mouth and sucking him hard and deep. He bobbed over the other man, cheering internally when Ransom's hands flew to his head and held him still as he began to fuck Levi's face instead.

It didn't take more than five or six full passes to get him totally hard.

Damn, it stretched his jaw wide and made him proud that he could take most of Ransom's cock.

It also made him eager, when Ransom grabbed the bottle of coconut oil that Rivet used for who-knew-what and slathered his hands with it before ordering, "Get up. Turn around."

Hell yes. It had been forever since they'd done this. Succumbed to their need for a quick and desperate fuck, intent on making each other explode as hard and fast as possible to avoid being caught. The thrill of their liaisons made them that much more powerful. Or at least that's the reason he told himself he loved coming together with Ransom so damn much.

Levi scrambled to his feet, nearly cracking his skull open when he slipped and not giving a single fuck. It would be worth it to feel Ransom buried inside him, gripping his hips and holding him steady while he rocked Levi's world.

Sure enough, Ransom's hands flashed out to anchor him until he got into place, bent at the waist, his hands braced on the shower wall, his ass up and out for Ransom to do whatever he pleased with it. His fingers were there instantly, parting Levi's cheeks and searching for his hole, which he coated in the organic oil.

Then he probed deeper, his fingers pressing inside a few times before they were replaced by the fat, blunt head of his dick. They didn't have time to take things slow, which was fine with him. "Yeah. Do it, Ransom."

This was the part where the other guy would have usually smacked his ass and reminded him who was in charge. That night, he didn't argue. It was as if he needed it just as bad as Levi. If so, Levi was happy to help his friend regain his own center.

Ransom fit his cock to Levi and worked it inside, making him groan. But when the other man hesitated, Levi didn't. He rocked backward, embedding Ransom within him in a single fluid movement.

"Fuck, you're so hot." Ransom reached down and gripped Levi's shoulder, tying them together.

He kept Levi close, refusing to allow him to move or fuck himself on Ransom's cock until he'd had a moment or two to adjust to the intrusion. When his ass relaxed a tiny bit around Ransom's shaft, the other man began to move.

Not delicately, but with a strength and decisiveness that made Levi's problems begin to disappear, replaced by pleasure. His cock swung beneath him, making him reach between his legs to fondle his own aching erection. Except Ransom knocked his hand away and replaced it with his own.

Levi certainly wasn't about to object. He needed relief, some way to vent the pressure building inside of him. Ransom promised, with every thrust deep into his body and jerk of his cock, that he would provide it.

Until a rap on the door had them both freezing in place. Like statues in the rain, they stood stock still as Rivet's voice twined around them. "Sorry, Levi. I gotta pee. I had too much coffee to get me through that."

She dashed into the bathroom. As soon as she spied Ransom plowing into Levi, she stumbled. But she didn't turn around and certainly didn't cover her eyes or retreat. No, she flat out stared.

"You like what you see?" Ransom asked her, his voice extra gravelly.

Oh shit, he liked being watched, did he? Levi's cock pulsed in Ransom's grip.

Rivet bit her lip, then nodded.

"Do what you came in here for," Ransom instructed.

"I'll leave you to it. Right. Sorry." Rivet was obscured behind the half-drawn curtain, at least lending her some privacy while she relieved herself. When the toilet flushed, Ransom yanked Levi out of the direct path of the water, which turned freezing then extra hot given the state of the ancient plumbing in their shitty apartment.

Except, when Rivet poked her head around the edge of the curtain, Ransom said, "I wasn't telling you to get out."

"You weren't?" Levi wondered, his ass clamping on Ransom's dick, making the other man groan.

"No," Ransom told them both. "We all need some relief after what happened earlier."

Ransom gestured around the bathroom and pretended to swipe it with the scanner. A little late but, yeah, they should probably figure out if they'd already fucked themselves. Fortunately Rivet was decent at charades. She nodded, sprinted toward the dining room and returned, sweeping the entire thing before placing the device outside the room, safe from the billowing cloud of steam surrounding them.

"Shut the door," Ransom commanded.

While he waited for Rivet to obey, he continued to fuck Levi though with short jabs instead of the wild lunges he'd been ramming into him with earlier. He was keeping them both revved while waiting for Rivet to catch up.

Levi let his mind blank and allowed Ransom to use his body to please them both. It was the best therapy he'd ever had in his life, permitting him to fly free without worry. To experience pleasure and be sure that he was giving just as much joy to his lovers.

Because that's what they were.

Physically connected or not, they were bonded. A trio.

Their shared experience had caused an unbreakable bond to develop between them. It would only make sex that much more intense and enjoyable.

Levi couldn't stop the strangled noise that left his throat as he watched Rivet take a step closer and then another. She rubbed her chest as if it ached and then smoothed her palms down her stomach to her mound.

"Yeah, we're going to take care of you," Ransom promised. "Get undressed. Quickly. I can't do this all day, no matter how much I wish I could."

Rivet already had her shirt off by the time he finished directing her to strip. She hopped out of her jeans, flashing her tight ass and slender, creamy thighs. Son of a bitch, how had he ever mistaken her for a dude?

Levi's cock twitched in Ransom's fist.

"She is beautiful, isn't she?" Ransom growled, making Rivet jerk her stare to them.

As if she didn't know how to take a compliment, or maybe didn't believe it for some dumb reason, she dropped to her knees on the bathmat and looked up at Levi, bracing her hand on his thigh. "You want me to suck you off while he's fucking you?"

Shit yes, he did. But he wasn't that selfish. Or maybe he was...because what he *really* wanted was to taste her and make her scream while Ransom worked his magic. He had to know that he had the power to make someone he loved happy instead of only ever hurting them.

Ransom and Rivet were his anchors. They were his family. They were everything he had left.

If he couldn't make them feel good and be happy, then what was the point of all this?

"Get up, Rivet," Ransom barked, and she did, without question. It was so odd to see her acquiesce, when she was feisty, rebellious, and independent any time other than when they were fooling around. Then again, Levi knew how she felt. Ransom was the only man he'd bent over for in his life.

Sure, he'd always been bisexual, but he'd never enjoyed being submissive until Ransom had put him in his very welcome place.

"Put one foot on the tub." Ransom reached down to grab the back of her knee and steady her, while still clamping Levi to him, Ransom's pelvis pinned to Levi's ass.

Levi knew exactly what Ransom had in mind as if they had shared his earlier thought telepathically. It was pretty obvious when Rivet's pretty pink pussy spread right in front of his face.

He licked his lips a moment before Ransom grabbed his hair and used the hold to direct his head between her legs. "Do a good job, Levi. Every time you make her cry out, I'm going to fuck you harder. Make her come and I'll do the same for you."

That was a deal. He would have told Ransom so if his mouth hadn't been full of Rivet.

He licked and sucked, tasted and teased, all while she cursed and called out his name.

Contorted, he relished the discomfort as if it made it okay for him to enjoy the rapture he felt being pinned between Ransom's thick cock and Rivet's sweet pussy. If getting off on this meant he was going to hell, he figured at least it would be for something that brought them pleasure too.

Worth it.

Ransom paced himself, fucking Levi with slow, thorough strokes that forced Levi's mouth tighter against Rivet's flesh each time he bottomed out. As Rivet's pussy coated his face with slickness and her cries grew louder and more unrestrained, Levi switched tactics, using his tongue to flick across her clit.

She quaked, causing him to reach out one hand to encircle the back of her slender thigh.

"Yes, that's right," Ransom told her. "Levi's got you. Why don't you show him how much you like what he's doing?"

"How?" she asked, her voice breathy with desire and an eagerness to do what he requested.

"By coming on his face." Ransom chuckled, a little too good at this for Levi to have any chance at withholding his own mounting bliss.

"Yeah." She nodded, biting her lower lip. "Close. Going to. Soon."

"Good." Ransom grunted, sinking deeper than before into Levi's ass. He wasn't unaffected by their display either.

Levi clenched around his partner, trying to influence him to join them. He should have known better. Ransom smacked his ass. Hard. "Don't tempt me. I'm not ready to be done with you two."

Oh, fuck. Did he plan to fuck Rivet too?

Levi's cock twitched, dripping precome as Ransom's fist shuttled over it.

Rivet's eyes began to close and her pussy tensed against his lips. He shifted his hand so that his fingers could reach farther upward. It wasn't the best angle, but he was able to slip two fingers an inch or two inside her as he continued to eat her out and absorb Ransom's fucking.

It might have been the best moment of his life, connected to not just one but two people he respected and desired. It must have ranked up there on Rivet's too.

Her eyes flew open wide, and she looked between Levi and Ransom.

Ransom nodded. "Go ahead."

He'd barely finished giving her permission when she crested.

Rivet screamed Levi's name and yanked his hair as she lost control. Her pussy spasmed around his fingers, smothering them with her heat and slickness. It was more than he could stand.

Ransom pumped into him from behind, hitting his prostate on every pass, making his balls swing heavily beneath him. His hand kept time with his thrusts, fucking Levi from the outside as well as the inside.

"Come with her, Levi," he growled. "Don't let her fall alone."

Rivet stared down at them, her mouth open in a distorted O as she rode the waves of her epic orgasm. Ransom steadied her with one beefy hand on her shoulder, while Levi did what he could with his hand on her hip. He was afraid he might have gripped her hard enough to bruise when his body responded to Ransom's demands.

He jerked then froze, hanging on the precipice of his orgasm.

Rivet tipped him over the edge when she smiled down at him and moaned. The redoubled pressure of her pussy clamping on his hand made him positive she liked what she saw and that she hoped to see more.

So he put on as good a show for her as he could.

He reared up, his mouth leaving her flesh with a wet sound.

Ransom changed the angle of his relentless pistoning, and that was all it took.

Come flew from his dick, splattering on his chest in pearly strands as Ransom milked him and Rivet looked on. She reached out, spreading the proof of his passion across his muscles, massaging it into his damp skin. And when another powerful blast tagged her wrist, Ransom released her shoulder to bring it to his lips.

He kissed the inside of her wrist, making her shudder again as he lapped Levi's release from the sensitive spot over her pounding pulse.

It was like a never-ending chain of pleasure, hers extending his and his doing the same for hers. It seemed to last forever, until Levi realized that Ransom was still rock hard in his ass.

Why hadn't he joined them?

Levi glanced over his shoulder with a raised brow.

"I want you both." He grimaced. "I need her too."

Levi nodded, then pulled away from Ransom. They both groaned when Ransom's dick slipped from his body. His legs still rubbery, Levi used the edge of the tub and then the sink as handholds so that he could reach the stash of condoms they kept in the medicine cabinet.

"Here, I owed you one," he said with a smile. Then he tossed the foil packet to Ransom, wrapped himself in one of their oversized towels, and sank to the floor. He reached for Rivet, drawing her down between his legs with her back to his chest. He hugged her tight and whispered in her ear. "Thank you for accepting me."

"Thank you for giving me the best orgasm of my life. Well, okay, it was tied with the one from the hotel." She smiled bashfully, making his head spin. Who was this woman and what had she done with the Rivet they knew? She was sweet and still innocent in some ways, something he never would have accused her of before.

"I have a feeling I'm not going to hold the record for long." Levi grinned and kissed her as Ransom rolled the latex down his huge erection and stepped out of the shower. Still dripping water, he seemed like some sort of elemental god, there to claim them both for his lascivious purposes.

Rivet's eyes widened, and she gasped, "Oh."

16

Ransom laughed. That bastard actually had the balls to stand there and chuckle as he took in the sight of Levi and Rivet cuddled on the antique black-and-white tiles of their bathroom. Good thing they kept the place spotless.

"I want to...uh...help you with that." Rivet waved her hand toward his cock, which hung low between his legs, swaying as he neared.

"Good, because I'm not done fucking yet." His mouth pulled tight, still needy and tense where Levi was liquid relaxation.

"I just...I hope you're not offended if I don't..." She looked up at Levi. "He did a really good job."

"Is that some kind of challenge?" Ransom's mouth kicked up on one side, making Levi's heart stutter. If it hadn't been intended as one, it was now. The man was relentless and there was no way any of them were leaving this bathroom until Rivet had come again, likely more than once.

Levi was game for that.

He snaked his hand around her to cup her breasts, as he'd figured out what she liked best that night in the hotel, which seemed like forever ago now. Rivet sighed and shifted, her ass rubbing against his cock, which hadn't fully softened yet. Damn, if she kept doing that he was going to have to go for another round himself.

Ransom's eyes dilated as he watched them feeding off each other's energy.

Levi leaned forward until he could take Rivet's legs in hand. They were thin enough that he could cradle the back of each thigh in one palm. Then he spread her apart, lifting her legs so they were draped over the outsides of his knees. The motion created plenty of space for Ransom, which he took advantage of.

He crouched, then went to his knees between theirs, crawling forward until his cock nudged Rivet's slightly concave belly, between her protruding hip bones. She was gorgeous, that was true, but Levi imagined what she would look like at her normal, healthy weight and couldn't resist tipping his head inward to skate his teeth over her neck at the thought.

Careful not to mark her anywhere visible, he forced himself to kiss her instead of sucking or biting the slender column of her neck.

"Oh shit. Okay." Rivet moaned, then reached for Ransom. "You're right. I want more too. Fuck me, Ransom."

Levi chuckled. That hadn't taken long at all. She was passionate and responsive and if the conditions had been different, he was sure they could take turns making her unravel all night long.

They'd have to settle for one more earthshattering orgasm, though.

Hell, they'd already risked getting caught too long. But he wasn't about to stop Ransom and Rivet from joining when he saw how much they needed each other and the release he'd already experienced at Ransom's hands...and cock.

Rivet squirmed in Levi's hold, angling her hips upward so it was easier for Ransom to fuse them.

"Don't rush me," Ransom told her sternly. "All you've had today are Levi's fingers, and maybe only your smaller ones for a while before that. I don't want to hurt you."

"You could never." Rivet reached for him, circling his cock with her fingers.

Levi winced. Ransom did look huge in her grasp.

Hell, he was impressive. His own ass stung after being stretched around Ransom. He didn't mind the burn, though. It reminded him that they'd so recently been locked together. One.

"Sometimes we hurt the people we try most not to." Ransom looked at them both then. "I hope this isn't one of those times."

Levi knew he wasn't talking about physical pain but the danger they were putting themselves in—bodies and hearts—by taking things between them one step further. Too late now. There was no stopping it.

Then there was no more talking about it either, because Ransom used two fingers on the top of his dick to angle it downward. He leaned forward and the blunt tip probed Rivet's tight, wet pussy.

She sighed and dropped her head on Levi's shoulder, making him proud she trusted him and relied on him to take care of her while she was mindless with bliss. He stroked the outsides of her legs, then ran his hands up her sides until he could play with her tits again, entertaining them both.

It also distracted her when Ransom edged forward, spreading her around his fat cock.

The big guy grunted when he lodged the barest bit inside her, unable to move forward without first retreating then trying again. He coated himself in her natural lubrication, sinking deeper with each pass. And when she held most of him, he stopped, cursing.

"Too good?" Levi asked with a grin. He remembered every moment he'd spent inside her that night in the motel before they'd rejoined Wildfire, and he'd give anything to do it again.

"So fucking good," Ransom agreed. "Why don't you play with her clit? I'm going to need some help here or I'm just going to tease her, get her worked back up, and end up disappointing her when I can't hold out for her to join me."

"I've got you covered, either way." Levi would be glad to go back for seconds if Ransom couldn't finish the job.

"Fuck you, I'm going to take care of this. Of her." The man seemed almost offended, reminding Levi that Ransom had scars of his own, even if he didn't show them as often.

"You're both doing a great job of that." She smiled up at them, half-satisfied from the orgasm Levi had given her, yet open to accepting more from Ransom.

"Not yet." Ransom leaned in, bracing his hand on the wall behind Levi. "But I will soon."

This time when he thrust into Rivet, he plunged even deeper, making her scoot upward on Levi's chest a full inch or two. She groaned, though not in pain.

"You like that, don't you?" Levi murmured in her ear. "Doesn't it feel amazing when he fills you?"

"Yes. Fuck yes." She angled her head, searching for his mouth with hers even as she reached for Ransom simultaneously.

Levi wasn't about to deny her. He sealed their lips and began to kiss her with languid caresses that complemented the slow press of Ransom's dick as he started to move more steadily within her.

Rivet gasped, her eyes losing some of their focus. But when Levi paused to ensure she was okay, she whimpered, then returned to making out with him with a passion he hadn't realized she possessed before. Rivet came alive in his arms, her hips rocking up to meet Ransom's.

The way she used his legs for leverage to squirm closer to his best friend's fucking only turned Levi on more. He slid his hands down her stomach then grabbed her ass, lifting her and helping her to grind on Ransom, making sure she took him as deep as possible.

It was like fucking Ransom in a whole new way.

"Quit torturing me and help her come instead," Ransom barked, though the taut lines at the sides of his neck and his straining muscles made it obvious he enjoyed what they were doing a hell of a lot.

Levi couldn't help but grin. "Oh yeah, I forgot."

"Don't make me put you over my knee later." Ransom would probably do it too. Somehow Levi didn't think Ransom's big hand spanking him would be much of a deterrent.

Rivet moaned at that, drawing the men's attention to her. Could she be into it too? He shouldn't be surprised anymore. The three of them seemed compatible in every possible way, at least when it came to bedroom activities.

So Levi cradled her, one arm wrapping around her waist to hold her steady while his opposite hand snaked across her hip, heading straight for her clit. When the pad of his index finger probed her soaked slit and traced it upward, she tensed.

As soon as he connected with her clit, she cried out his name, then Ransom's.

Ransom gritted his teeth and began to thrust into her with long, steady strokes that shook all three of them. Levi knew it wasn't the kind of lovemaking that would last long. No, it was a fast, intense rush of rapture that would burn bright and extinguish quickly.

So he began to rub small circles there in time to Ransom's shuttling between her legs. Every once in a while he split his fingers and massaged her pussy around Ransom's plunging cock, awed by how wide he was spreading her satiny flesh and how well Rivet was taking it.

When Rivet's steady moans and cries turned silent and her breathing grew ragged, he knew she was close. So he gave Ransom, who was understandably distracted by the clasp of her clenching muscles around him, a heads up. "Come on, Ransom. Give it to her. She's almost there. Fuck her harder. Faster."

"Fly with me," Rivet whispered. It wasn't a command, though. More like a request. A need to not be alone that resonated deep within Levi. "Please, Ransom."

If she was going to make herself vulnerable, she needed someone else to do the same or she wouldn't be able to enjoy being so exposed.

"You're so amazing, Rivet," he whispered in her ear.

"So brave. You can do this. Come apart. I've got you."

It was what Ransom had told him earlier. It healed part of Levi's fractured soul that he could give her what Ransom gave him. A steady place to rest, shelter from the storm around them, and hope that things could maybe... possibly...if only for a few moments...get better instead of worse.

"Thank you," she gasped, then fused their mouths again. Their tongues met and danced over each other. He mimicked the motion with his finger on her clit. She showed him exactly how she needed to be touched in order to explode.

Ransom groaned. "Fuck, yes. You're getting so tight on me I can hardly fucking move."

He was doing his best, though, nearly making Levi's teeth rattle as he absorbed the impact of his best friend's thrusts into their lover. To be so involved in their pleasure amped Levi up too.

His cock had gotten hard again and was sliding between the cheeks of Rivet's ass, making him wonder what it would be like to have her sandwiched between him and Ransom, both of them buried inside her welcoming body together.

Would he be able to feel Ransom's cock sliding in and out of her through the delicate tissue that would separate them if he buried himself in her ass right then?

Probably, though he wouldn't get to find out. At least not right then. The two of them were too far gone to slow down now.

Ransom plowed into Rivet, his body a graceful machine intent on bringing her the maximum amount of bliss possible. His shoulders bunched and his ass clenched as he drove into her over and over. Levi played with her clit while he kissed the shit out of her, and when he slid his hand upward from her waist to her breasts and pinched one of her nipples, she shuddered.

So he did it again, and again...even harder this time.

Rivet's eyes flew open and she stared straight into his as she went over the edge. He held her tight, keeping her close as he'd promised when she finally gave in to the onslaught of sensations.

"Ransom..." he warned his partner, though he didn't have to.

"I feel it. Oh, fuck. She's so fucking tight. Wet. So good. I'm going to shoot. Can't stop it." He groaned, deep and guttural, the sound reverberating off the tile walls.

In response, Rivet jerked harder, her orgasm shaking every bit of her. Even her toes curled where they'd come to rest on top of his knees. Every bit of her reacted to Ransom within her, possessing her, giving her everything he had.

And to Levi's manipulations too. He felt her pussy spasming beneath his fingers, drawing every drop of fluid from Ransom's balls.

His partner shouted then froze before surrendering to a final frenzy of fucking. And when he locked as deeply as possible and ground against Rivet, he trapped Levi's hand in place, making it an extension of his own body, doing whatever was necessary to grant Rivet the release she so desperately needed.

Hell, all of them did.

And when Rivet collapsed, floppy in his arms, Levi felt something more powerful than the lust that had coursed through him earlier. He felt tenderness, and compassion, and...something warm that spread throughout his chest, scaring the ever-loving shit out of him.

No. It wasn't possible.

He was never making that mistake again.

Trying not to panic, he allowed the bulk of Ransom's huge frame in addition to Rivet's much more slender one act like a weighted blanket, calming his mind as he cushioned them both, saving them from the harsh realities of the cold, hard floor.

But neither of them were having that for long.

As soon as he could think and breathe again, Ransom shifted. He put his fingers on the base of the condom sheathing his softening cock and withdrew from Rivet's body. She whimpered at the loss and Levi knew exactly how she felt, because he missed being joined with the man just as much.

Damn, he'd filled that condom up. They were lucky it hadn't burst or overflowed.

Levi tried not to be a little jealous, wondering if it was because Ransom wasn't settling for some guy's ass instead of a woman's pussy, which he obviously preferred.

Ransom must have caught his appreciative glance. "Hey, can't blame me. I've been storing that up for a while and I finally got to fuck you both."

His satisfied rasp hit Levi right in the feels, even if he wished he could stop that from happening. It was obvious to him now, with both of these people, he was defenseless. At their mercy.

So when Rivet tattled on him, he knew he was going to be in for it. "Ransom, he's hard again. His cock is jabbing me in the back."

"Is it, really?" Ransom's crooked smile did nothing to make him less turned on, that was for sure.

"Yup." Rivet nodded, then stretched lazily before spinning in his arms so that she draped over his chest. She kissed his shoulder, then his neck, and finally sat on her heels between his legs when she asked him, "What should we do about that?"

"Ignore it." Levi covered himself with his hand. Or at least he tried. His cock was so fucking hard you would have thought it had been months since he'd come and not only minutes.

Ransom nudged Rivet to one side, spreading Levi's legs apart almost uncomfortably wide to make room for himself beside her.

"I don't think so." He swiped Levi's fingers away and replaced them with his own.

Levi lurched as though he'd stuck his dick in the socket instead of Ransom's fist. But the guy knew exactly how to touch him, stroke him, jerk him off like he had earlier.

Rivet said, "He already came like that before. I think he deserves something better."

"Me too." Ransom licked his lips.

Could he...?

When he lowered himself to the ground, his face inches from Levi's cock, Levi scooted backward. "You don't have to do that."

"I will if you don't want to." Rivet hummed. She made more room for Ransom by straddling Levi's thigh, which of course meant that her bare, wet pussy was pressed against him. She sighed as she watched Ransom edging nearer, then began to rub herself on Levi as if she hadn't already come too...twice.

How lucky was he that both his lovers were as insatiable as him? Ordinarily, he'd say very, but right then he was scared of giving them too much more. He wasn't going to be able to close himself off again after this or lie to himself and say that their connection was merely physical.

And yet, he was weak.

He couldn't push them away. Didn't want to, deep down. Still, he tried one last time. "Seriously, Ransom…"

"Relax. I know I don't have to go down on you. I want to." Ransom nuzzled Levi's cock and balls, getting his face right in there. He certainly wasn't squeamish for a guy who hadn't ever thought of himself as anything but straight until life had forced him to see other possibilities.

"Have you ever sucked a cock before?" Levi asked, his heart racing even as he tried not to get his hopes up. He didn't want Ransom to do anything he was uncomfortable with.

"No. But maybe Rivet can give me some pointers." He smiled sheepishly at Rivet, who put her hand on his shoulder, squeezing him before leaning down to plant a kiss on his cheek.

"Of course I will." She slid back until she was riding the spot just above Levi's knee. He planted his foot against the tub so it was high enough to make it easier for her. She bent forward, moaning when she pressed against his angled thigh fully, then put her hand over Ransom's on Levi's dick, making a spurt of precome escape from the tip. "Why don't you start with that? Lick it off, lightly. Make your tongue flat and wide and soft to start."

Son of a bitch.

How was Levi supposed to last more than a single exploratory lick of Ransom's virgin tongue when Rivet was giving him naughty instructions like that? Ransom sucked in a deep breath, but any misgivings he had flew out the window when he followed Rivet's directions perfectly.

He chuckled as Levi stiffened, already struggling for some self-control.

Rivet noticed too. She laughed. "I'd say you're a natural. He's about to burst already."

"Can't help it that the two of you are sexy as sin and watching you fuck practically on top of me does magical things to my body."

"I don't blame you." Rivet shrugged one shoulder, her acceptance like a balm to him compared to Laurel's scorn. He scrunched his eyes closed, not wanting to think of his ex-wife right then. Or ever again, to be honest.

That, of course, made him remember what a piece of shit he really was, and his cock responded accordingly.

"Oh no." Ransom growled, then bit his thigh in warning. "I'm down here, and ready to suck my first cock. Don't freak out now."

Rivet smacked him lightly. "It's okay if he's not ready."

Levi was stuck between what he wanted and what he thought was right. But with Rivet holding the way out open for him, he realized he didn't want to go that direction. How much would he regret it for the rest of his life if he didn't take this opportunity the one and only time it was likely to present itself?

Ransom waited for him to nod. "Do it. Put me out of my misery already. I'm dying here."

They all knew he was talking about far more than physical relief. He needed to be mindless. He needed an excuse to allow himself to feel before he lost the ability to be human at all.

He wasn't a robot. He was a man.

Or at least he'd like to be again someday, even if it hurt.

"That's so good, Levi." Rivet rubbed his abs, making

them clench beneath her light caresses. "You sit back and let us take care of you."

He nodded, then closed his eyes, praying for some stamina.

"And you," she directed Ransom. "Get your mouth on him. Start slow and see how far you can take him without choking. Give yourself time to adjust."

Of course that fucker didn't listen well. He slid down Levi's shaft too fast and coughed. Even that first hint of heat and wetness sent shocks through Levi's body. His eyes flew open in time to see Rivet grab hold of Ransom's hair and pull him off.

Damn, that made his cock stiffen the rest of the way again.

"Try it again, but listen to me this time. Take it easy or you're going to make this all about you instead of giving him what he needs," Rivet lectured Ransom, making Levi shift restlessly. They were so fucking hot together he didn't stand a chance.

This time, when Ransom engulfed Levi's cock in his mouth, he did better. Took it gradually into the depths of his mouth until the head tucked against the back of his throat. And even then, he didn't stop, allowing Levi to press beyond until Ransom had him fully within his grasp.

"There you go." Rivet petted Ransom's head. "Now start sucking him. Softly. Concentrate on the tip. Think about what you like when he does it to you, then try that."

Oh shit! Levi's ass came off the ground as his partner began to explore.

He was good at this. Or maybe Rivet was an excellent teacher. Either way, he felt his eyes roll back. And when he was able to focus again, he realized that Rivet had slipped two fingers inside herself as she rode his leg.

He could at least help with that. He reached forward and probed her entrance with his larger digits, making her moan.

"Thanks, but these were for you. Not me." She grinned as she withdrew her soaked fingers.

When he realized what she intended, he groaned and spread his legs farther.

It took some adjusting, with Ransom pulling him closer so he slid down the wall, but eventually Rivet was able to find her mark. She rubbed his hole, then pressed inside, giving him something to clench around while Random blew him over and over.

"Ah, fuck," he groaned.

"Now, if you can reach, rub his balls. Tug a little while you swallow around him and prepare yourself. Before long, he's going to lose it. There's no way he can resist this trifecta. If you don't want him to come in your mouth, let me suck him instead."

Levi groaned and writhed between them. She was diabolical in the best possible sense.

His sac tightened in anticipation. There was no holding back. No prolonging this exquisite pleasure and pain any longer. Rivet was right. He was going to blow.

But he didn't expect his friend to drink his release. Not when he was new to this.

Ransom shocked him again, humming loud enough to vibrate Levi's entire shaft as if he relished the idea instead of being grossed out by it.

Rivet grinned and twined her fingers in the hair at the back of Ransom's head. "Yeah, that's right. Make him come and enjoy every drop."

Levi's eyes widened. Who knew Rivet had *that* in her? He supposed he should have since she was tough, and courageous, and bold. But damn!

Hearing her get bossy with Ransom was the last straw. He arched, his head hitting the tile wall hard enough that it should have hurt. It didn't. No pain could penetrate the dome of arousal and ecstasy Ransom and Rivet had constructed around them with their affection and understanding and lust.

Levi stretched and stretched, then snapped.

His balls pulsed in Ransom's slightly too-firm grip. His ass tightened around Rivet's fingers. Then his dick pulsed as his release tore through him. He emptied himself into Ransom's greedy, still-sucking mouth.

"Yeah, that's it." Rivet was there, petting his chest, returning the favor by biting his nipple and sucking on it like he'd pinched hers earlier. All the while, she talked him through the most intense climax of his life. "Give him all of it. Show him how much you like it and how good of a job he did for his first time."

A strangled shout ripped from Levi's chest. Hell, it might have come straight from his soul.

Rivet got him. And so did Ransom. They understood pain and loss and grief and how badly he needed this relief, even if it was a temporary reprieve. He was sure, in that moment, that he loved them both.

Which meant he was completely fucked. Because if he didn't protect them and help them get through this mess whole, he would have failed again. Worse this time, because he should have known better than to leave his heart unprotected.

As if his pleasure impacted them both, Rivet jerked her hips several times, using his thigh to get herself off.

She whisper-screamed his name as they came together. And before he realized what was happening, Ransom did the same. He jammed one hand beneath himself, surely tugging on his cock before moaning and making a mess of the tiles even as he finished drinking Levi down.

Levi collapsed, floating in the wake of his climax.

At some point, Ransom must have regained his wits because Levi realized the other man had propped himself against the tub and was pulling Levi and Rivet to him, one on each side. They crashed into him, Levi tucked under one arm and Rivet the other. She curled up into a tight ball that made her seem even more petite than she actually was.

They sat there, huddled together, until Levi's legs went numb and his ass was freezing where it was glued to the tiles.

"I wish we could take this to a nice, comfortable, clean bed." Ransom sighed as he surveyed his two lovers. For the first time since he'd joined Levi in the bathroom, a grimace tugged at the corners of his lips.

"Maybe we could…" Levi began to propose before shaking his head. Stupid.

"It's too risky." Rivet shook her head. At least she still had a few brain cells functioning. "In fact, we've already stayed in here too long together already. What if they have heat sensors? The steam from the shower might have blacked this room out temporarily, but it won't for much longer. I can't be responsible for you two getting made. Not when we're so close to the end."

"She's right." Ransom stood, then held one hand out to each of them. Levi took what last contact he could by placing his palm against Ransom's. Rivet did the same.

The guy pulled them to their feet as if they weighed

nothing. Yet Levi would have to do without his best friend's strength during the long, cold night.

"Well..." He shrugged. "Thanks for keeping me from losing my mind. It's been fun."

It seemed so inadequate for everything he was feeling at the moment, and not only because he was high on endorphins. His emotions ran deep, yet he knew better than to admit it out loud.

Rivet nodded and shot him a sad smile before snugging a towel around her torso, collecting her clothes and the shapewear she used to conceal her true self, and slinking away to her spot on the couch. He hated to let her go. Hated that her status as the newest full member meant they hadn't been able to give up their room for her. She slept closest to the door, which wasn't ideal in case someone entered. Levi hated that he couldn't protect her or smother her with the affection she craved and deserved.

Worse, he hated sharing the only bedroom in their apartment with Ransom yet being so far away.

As he stared up from the bottom bunk of their surplus military cots at the exposed coils of Ransom's berth, he wondered if this was how the other man had felt all the nights he'd gone to bed in prison—trapped, claustrophobic, and doomed by the things he had no control over in his life.

Levi could only hope they weren't waiting out a death sentence.

Though if they were, at least he'd stolen one last taste of pleasure and connection. Devouring Ransom and Rivet had been far better than anything he could have requested for a last meal.

17

By seven o'clock the next morning Ransom had tossed and turned for so many hours, he couldn't stand to lie there and pretend to sleep another moment, not even to make sure Levi was still breathing slow and easily as he dozed.

At least one of them had been able to get some rest.

He hoped Rivet had done the same. Unable to quit worrying about her, out in the living room by herself, he rolled from bed with minimal squeaking of the metal frame and made a pit stop by the bathroom. It took a minute to get his morning wood under control, especially since he'd never be able to stand in that room without remembering what they'd done there. When he finished, he headed down the hall.

How could one single day have held some of both the best and worst moments he'd ever experienced? The live horror show Angus had put on for them had been followed up by the most incredible sex he'd ever had. Things were escalating and every emotion seemed so intense it was giving him mental whiplash.

Maybe adrenaline had something to do with how deeply he'd felt their physical intimacy the night before, but he didn't think so. There was something more powerful at play.

How else was it possible that after they'd fucked, Levi had actually dropped into a deep sleep despite the trauma he'd endured only hours before? That had to mean something. Maybe when this was over, hopefully very soon, they could find a way to make this thing work between them.

Or maybe he'd lose the two people he'd come to enjoy and rely on as if they were extensions of himself. He shivered despite the fact that they'd bumped the thermostat up a full five degrees now that Rivet was bunking out in the living room, next to the drafty door.

When Ransom shuffled to the couch, where she was curled up, only occupying two-thirds of the space, he took the blanket from the back of the cushion and draped it over her, tucking her in. In her sleep, she smiled and nuzzled into his touch. So he stood there, staring down at her as he ran his hand over her shorn hair.

Seeing her wearing that long wig at Jordan's place had put the vision in his mind and he imagined her, six months from now or maybe even six years from now, as her natural beauty was allowed to blossom instead of being stifled in the name of whatever the fuck they were doing.

If she preferred herself like this, he'd have no problem with it. She was sexy as fuck as is.

But it had been clear in her confident strut and her gleaming smile that Sevan was the person she truly was and longed to be again, as soon as they finished their assignment.

Three days.

They might only have seventy-two hours left together. Fuck his life.

After two years of hoping every day for their big break, they had the opportunity they'd waited so long for, and suddenly it seemed like he wanted to savor every moment in between now and then. How fucked up was that?

Ransom tore himself away, moving into the kitchen where he brewed enough coffee for the three of them. He leaned his hip against the counter, sipping his first cup while searching for a pancake recipe on his phone's internet browser. If he only had a few more tries to make a good enough impression on Rivet and Levi that they might not bail on him, if he was even allowed to walk free...

His hand clamped so hard at the possibility that this could end in something other than a clusterfuck of epic proportions that his mug cracked, sloshing hot coffee all over him. "Ow. Shit. Fuck. Damn."

"Everything okay?" Rivet asked groggily.

"Peachy," he responded, irritated that he'd disturbed her in the process of scalding the shit out of his fingers.

She staggered into the kitchen in time to spy the mess he'd made. While he ran his hand under cold water, she grabbed a towel and began to mop the floor on her hands and knees.

"I'll get that." He used his foot to try to shoo her away, or at least to get her to stand up instead of crawling around on the ground because of him. She didn't belong there. Would he always bring down those around him?

"Don't be silly. It's fine." She finished and tossed the towel on the counter before reaching for a fresh one from the drawer. Instead of hanging it on the stove handle like they usually did, she retrieved several ice cubes from the freezer and wrapped them in the fabric instead.

She came close enough that he could smell her shampoo and the coconut oil she used on her skin. Of course, that only reminded him of fucking Levi and he started to get hard.

He hoped she wouldn't notice when she nudged his bicep. "Let me see."

"It's nothing." He shook his head, but she took his wrist anyway, inspecting the red splatter marks before wrapping it gingerly with the makeshift icepack.

Ransom didn't complain too much when she held his hand, enjoying the connection even if it was merely temporary.

She sighed and looked up at him. "Can I ask you something?"

"What more is there I haven't already told you?" He grimaced as he recalled spilling his darkest secrets and how they hadn't kept her from going pliant in his arms. Right before Angus had ruined the moment. That bastard.

"Why do you go by Ransom?" She leaned in. "I mean, I get that you can't use your real name, but why that? Did you pick it?"

How the hell did she see right to the heart of him so easily?

"Yeah, I did." He shrugged. Might as well be honest. "Ransom is what you pay to get a person or possession of value back from someone evil."

Rivet thought about that for a moment before she frowned and nodded. "You're trying to exchange your time, and possibly your life, in order to get...what? Yourself? Your freedom?"

"Maybe I thought it could be my ticket out of hell, or

even purgatory." He shrugged one shoulder so he wouldn't disturb the spot where they were joined. It wasn't the stupidest idea he'd ever had. "Just like Levi last night, I'd like to have the chance to do things differently this time around."

"I want to be on the right side of this fight too." Rivet laid her head on his chest.

So he put his free arm around her and squeezed. "How about we forget that shit today and just hang out? You, me, and Levi."

"Probably best if we try to keep the nerves at bay. It could be a long fucking three days." She winced when she said *fucking*. That wasn't what he'd had in mind, but he wasn't an idiot. If they got naked together again, he wasn't going to say no. Not when they could soon be ripped apart, or worse...

"Food first. You need energy to make it through. Do you like pancakes?" he asked.

Her stomach answered for her, growling loudly. They both laughed.

"Thanks for the first aid." He reluctantly retrieved his hand from hers so he could get to work. "I think I'm good to go now."

Rivet smiled up at him. "Can I help?"

"Do *you* know how to cook?" He stared down at her, wondering if she'd been holding out this whole time.

"Hell no, but we can practice together, right?" She hesitated. "I take direction well. Unless you want to do it by yourself."

"Anything I do with you is more fun. Come on." He reached into the container of flour on the counter, then flung a bit in her direction.

Rivet laughed and said, "Let's make Levi breakfast in bed."

Ransom had never had such a perfect plan. Unless it was that they have Levi for breakfast instead. He imagined drizzling syrup over the man and watching Rivet lick it off. Which of course meant he had to adjust himself. That only set Rivet off again.

When he glanced down he realized he'd left a giant white handprint over his junk on his black shorts. Oops. He shrugged, then got busy whipping together the batter with Rivet's assistance.

They made it as far as melting butter in the frying pan and adding dollops of the batter to it when she circled back to their previous discussion. He was staring at the pancakes and the bubbles forming in them when Rivet asked, "What's your real name?"

He didn't respond right away.

"Come on, you know mine. It's only fair." Rivet pressed herself full length against his side and looped her arms around his waist. She was extremely persuasive.

He looked down at her and said, "Craig. Craig Ivers."

"Nice to meet you, Craig." She went up on her tiptoes then and kissed him sweetly.

Both of them forgot to keep an eye on the pancakes as the exchange turned steamy in a hurry. They were full on making out, just like they had been on the couch the night before, when the smoke alarm started blaring a shrill alert.

"Son of a bitch!" he roared, and whipped his shirt off, using it to fan the air in front of the device while Rivet cracked up and took the frying pan to the sink. The first two pancakes looked and sounded more like hockey pucks than anything edible as she dumped them out.

Levi sprinted into the room, his hair totally mussed, his shorts barely hanging on to his hipbones, and his chest and feet bare. Despite the rude awakening, he was ready to fight. For them.

When he realized the commotion was only Ransom fucking up in the kitchen again instead of something life-threatening, he grinned and poured himself a cup of coffee.

"Shit. We were going to surprise you," Rivet grumbled. "Except I sort of distracted Ransom and then... Oops."

Levi's smile widened. "Distracted him how exactly?"

"By kissing the shit out of him." Rivet reflected his joy. It made Ransom's heart skip to see them both happy and relaxed. So even though they shouldn't, he knew he wasn't going to stop what was about to happen.

"Well, that sounds more appealing to me than food at the moment." Levi practically purred as he reached one hand out to each of them. He was like sex incarnate, that man. Sensual and open, he made it possible for Ransom to take anything he needed.

And right now, that was both of his roommates.

"It says you can refrigerate the batter and use it whenever you're ready," Rivet added helpfully, already tucking the bowl into the fridge.

"Perfect." Levi snagged her around her waist, then pinned her against the appliance. "Because I think I need an appetizer before we get to those."

"Sounds good to me." Rivet licked her lips. Then she looked at Ransom, "You in, Craig?"

"You told her?" Levi's eyes went wide. Not because he was pissed that Ransom had breached their confidentiality, but because he knew what that meant. Ransom trusted her completely, and thought of her as far more than a pawn in the dangerous game they were playing.

He nodded. "I'm in. All in."

18

Rivet wasn't about to give the universe any opportunity to interrupt what they were cooking between them now. She shimmied out of her sweats and peeled off her oversized T-shirt, grateful to shed the ill-fitting clothes.

The appreciative stares both Levi and Ransom gave her when she tossed them into a pile on the floor made her certain that they approved as well.

"I'll never get over that." Levi stepped nearer and ran the back of his hand from her neck down her chest between her breasts. "You're so fucking cute, and then I see the real you and you're...all this."

"Are you ever disappointed I'm not the guy you thought I was?" She cleared her throat and tried not to look away, but it was no use.

He lifted her chin and stared into her eyes when he said, "I couldn't give a fuck if you're a guy or a girl. It's *you* I'm attracted to. It's just that you were hiding so much of yourself I feel like I only got a hint of it before. Now..."

"It would be impossible to stay away now that we see you for you," Ransom added.

"Yeah, what he said." Levi kissed her nose while he shucked his shorts.

And then he took the last step remaining between them so she could feel his erection pressed against her stomach. He was ready and raring to go this morning.

"Didn't get enough last night?" she teased.

"I could never have enough of you two." Levi glanced up to include Ransom in his promise. The other man was hovering over her shoulder, the rustling of fabric telling her he wasn't about to let them have all the fun on their own. Yes!

Sure enough, Ransom wrapped his arms around her from behind. But he didn't close the circle with only her inside. Instead he extended them until he had a grip on Levi too. He smooshed them together as he hugged them both, drawing them as close to him as he could.

Rivet hummed as heat seeped into her and the pressure of their broad chests made her feel secure and safe. Something she hadn't felt in a long time. Maybe ever.

It was nearly as welcome as the pressure of Ransom's cock nudging the small of her back.

Damn, she had to feel him inside her again.

The night before he'd shown her what it was like to truly be fucked. What limited experience she had was nothing like what he'd done to her and she couldn't wait for him and Levi to do it again. At least if things went badly when they clashed with the Savage Skulls, she would have really lived first.

This one time, she intended to be selfish.

Take purely for her own enjoyment, and hopefully give them the same in return.

"Before we get too far down this road..." Ransom slid his hands along Levi's back and to her hips, separating them just a bit. Which was entirely too much as far as she was concerned.

"What now?" Levi groaned, and Rivet agreed wholeheartedly.

"I think we're out of condoms." His fingers tightened on her as if he was pissed about that fact.

"Well, I'm on continuous birth control." Rivet shrugged one shoulder. "It would be hard to explain if I suddenly got my period. So unless there's some other reason we shouldn't..."

"Not on my part." Levi shook his head.

"Mine either," Ransom practically growled. "Are you telling me we can fuck you bare?"

Rivet leaned her head back against his shoulder. "I already trust you with my life. Why should this be any different?"

"She's got a point there." Levi kissed her as if thanking her for her confidence. She had more in them than either man had in himself given their pasts. Same was true of them for her. And she wanted nothing more than to reward them for helping her remember that underneath the mountain of her doubts and fears, she could be strong. That together, they just might pull this off.

While Levi teased her lips, Ransom rocked against her, as if warming up for the similar arc he'd be making when he slid deep inside her. He watched closely as Levi riled her up. When Ransom tipped his head so he could kiss her neck, she shuddered.

"Does she like that?" He chuckled then did it again, careful not to leave a mark while weakening her knees with a swirl of his tongue on the sensitive skin beneath her ear.

"I'd say so," Levi confirmed, taking a break so they could both suck in a deep breath or two. "Her nipples are rock hard."

"Suck them," Ransom ordered, taking control as if he'd been having threesomes his whole adult life. It wasn't cheesy or awkward as he orchestrated their pleasure, so she conscientiously decided to stop thinking about everything in favor of feeling it and enjoying it to her full capability.

Levi didn't seem to have any complaints either. He did as he was told, taking one tight tip into his mouth and drawing on it before laving it with flicks of his talented tongue. Rivet's head lolled on Ransom's shoulder. She put one hand on Levi's biceps and the other behind her on Ransom's thigh, pulling them both as close to her as she could manage.

It still wasn't enough.

She tried to press her mound up against Levi's thigh, but he had his legs spread around hers. The best she could do was to rub herself on the length of his hard-on, wishing she had superpowers and could levitate right about then.

"You're ready for more?" Ransom correctly read her body language.

"Yeah." She hardly recognized her own voice, so breathy and full of lust.

"Are you sore from last night?" he asked.

Rivet would ordinarily have denied any discomfort due to sex or otherwise; it was a knee-jerk reaction. But for some reason, she came clean. It was easy to tell him the truth. She wasn't afraid he'd think less of her or override what she needed or consider her weak for it. "A little, but not enough to keep me from taking you, both of you. That's what I want. So give me your cock. Now."

He laughed, shaking her with the gentle movement. "Planning on it. As long as you'll tell me if it gets to be too much. I'm not sure I can hold myself back again like last night."

"Wait. That was your version of restrained?" Holy hell.

He did freeze then. "Yeah. Why? Too much?"

"No. It pisses me off that you held back, and it makes me curious." She looked up at Levi and smiled when she said. "Don't do that today. None of us should."

Levi nodded. Then he said, "Let me get you ready."

Ransom answered for her. "Good idea."

Then he kicked one of the tall stools out from beneath the table and sat on it where she would have had to hop or climb up. The chair back creaked when he leaned against it, but it was sturdy. At least she thought it would be up to what he obviously had in mind when he gathered her into his lap, her back still plastered to his chest.

Carefully, he arranged her so that she didn't crush his cock and balls. Her legs draped over his thick thighs, her feet naturally coming to rest on the spindles at the sides. They made a perfect footrest and place to brace herself, which was handy when Levi dropped to his knees between their spread legs and began kissing her pussy as enthusiastically as he had her mouth.

"Son of a bitch!" She bowed in Ransom's hold, but his arms, looped around her, ensured she wasn't going anywhere or crashing to the floor.

"Tell me when she's ready for me," Ransom instructed

Levi. While he used one arm to cradle her, he let his other hand roam from her knee to her inner thigh, then upward, petting her mound and stomach before cupping her breasts and weighing them in his palm.

Whatever Levi was doing to her was making it impossible for her to form coherent words, but they both seemed to understand her urgency when she moaned and writhed between them. Levi slipped two fingers inside, pressing with constant force until he was buried fully within her. He didn't have to work her open or lick his hand to add any lubrication; they were making her plenty wet on their own.

"There, see," she rasped to Ransom. "All good. Let's go."

He chuckled again, making her aware of how often he did it when she and Levi were chasing the shadows from his mind. She made it her goal to bring this side out of him as often as possible.

"Greedy." He nipped her earlobe, which did nothing to make her less horny.

She squeezed Levi's fingers within her, wishing it was one of their cocks instead.

And soon she would get her wish.

"I like that about you, Rivet." He looked down over her shoulder at Levi. "What do you think? Is she telling the truth or trying to rush us?"

"She's soaked," Levi confirmed. "I was just having too much fun to let go."

"I want to feel for myself." Ransom glided his hand lower again, but Levi didn't take his fingers from her. Ransom cupped her mound, pressing his fingers in beside his best friend and partner's.

Oh fuck, that was hot. Rivet moaned.

What would it be like if they fucked her at the same time? She wanted to find out. But maybe Ransom was right, she needed to work up to that.

After a couple pumps of his thick digits within her, he withdrew and fed them to Levi, who eagerly cleaned her fluids from them.

"That's right, Levi," he encouraged the other man. "You keep eating her while I fuck her. When she comes, you can have a turn."

Sounded great to Rivet. She arched her back and spread her legs wider, putting more weight on her feet so she could lift her ass and help Levi, who guided Ransom's cock toward her opening.

"Here I come," he told her as the blunt head of his cock notched against her core.

"Yes!" she shouted as she lowered herself, letting gravity do most of the work.

Ransom spread her pussy wide as she slid down his length until he was fully embedded within her body. She hugged him tight, her breath catching in her chest as he filled her completely.

And just when she thought it might be a little too much, Levi was there, massaging her, drawing circles around her clit with his tongue, and helping her enjoy blowing Ransom's mind every bit as much as he had done to her.

"Fuck, you feel so good on me. So hot and snug." He grunted as he clasped her hips and began to lift and lower her, using her body to stroke his erection. "Being in you bare is fucking amazing."

She would have told him it felt incredible to her too if

she could have concentrated on anything but the way her body conformed to his right then.

This wasn't going to be some long, drawn-out affair. Her body was ready for him. Eager for release already. She needed an orgasm to take the edge off so she could enjoy the rest of what they had in store for her more fully.

So she reached down and yanked Levi's head tighter to her pussy. She fucked his face even as Ransom fucked her. He didn't seem to mind, looking up at her with piercing blue eyes that shone with affection and desire.

"Ransom!" she called, and he understood the primal note in her request.

"Fuck yes, come on me. Come on Levi's face. Show him how much you love what he's doing and how much you can't wait until he's inside you, like I am now." Ransom whipped out his dirty talk. For a man so quiet she'd hardly heard him speak the past two years, he sure as shit saved his filthy mouth for the best possible use.

Rivet froze as every muscle in her body gathered. She clenched around him and hung there for a few seconds until the insistent rub of Levi's tongue took her over the edge. Her toes curled and she screamed as she came for them both, but mostly for herself.

When her eyes opened and she sucked in enough breaths that she thought she might not pass out after all, she realized her climax had squeezed Ransom from her body before he'd had a chance to join her. Levi was sucking on his balls and making the other man groan.

"Enough, Levi." Ransom waved him away. "Take for yourself. Get in there and fuck her. Get her ready for me again."

Was that possible? Rivet was about to tell him he'd lost

his damn mind, because she'd come so hard she was still seeing stars.

But when Levi stood, there was no denying him or the passion he directed at her.

Whether she could reach that peak again with him, or ever again in her life considering how high they'd boosted her, she wanted him to feel the same.

"You heard the man," she said in her best attempt at a sultry come-hither. "Get in here."

As if he could tell she was struggling to keep up with them, not in spirit but in body, Ransom reached down and shackled her ankles in his big hands. He lifted her feet so that one rested on each of his knees. He held her there, surprisingly comfortable against his frame.

The angle made it so she was almost reclining, giving Levi the perfect approach. He stood between their legs and stared at her pussy while he tugged on his own cock. It was longer than Ransom's if not as thick, plenty to drive her wild.

Especially now that she was already primed from the orgasm they'd given her together.

Levi fit himself to her and asked, "You sure this is okay?"

"It will be once you join us," she promised. "Hurry, please."

To her amazement, he reawakened her pleasure centers as he sank into her with ease. They both moaned as they fit together so perfectly. He took up where Ransom had left off, pumping into her slowly at first but increasing the pace when he realized she was as desperate as him to chase the next climax.

"Your balls are rubbing my dick while you fuck her,

you know that?" Ransom told him, making both Levi and Rivet pant. "You're not even trying and you're going to make me come if you're not careful."

"Not sorry," Levi said with a crooked smile an instant before he leaned forward and crushed his mouth to Ransom's.

Rivet turned her head so she could watch them make out while Levi's fucking turned more frantic. His hands clasped Ransom's upper arms for leverage as he plowed into her, taking her up, up again. When her pussy quivered around him, she knew it was only a matter of a few more strokes.

He broke his kiss with Ransom and murmured, "She's getting close."

So Ransom hummed his approval, then snaked his hand between her and Levi so he could play with her clit.

Oh shit. That felt too good to resist.

So she didn't.

Rivet threw her head back and moaned as she shattered on Levi's cock. He roared too, telling Ransom, "Going to come in her."

"Do it. Shoot." Ransom guaranteed it with his dirty talk. "Fill her up so I can feel it when I fuck her again."

When he what? Rivet couldn't be sure she heard him right as all the blood in her body was rushing through her veins. She hadn't even stopped shuddering when Levi pulled out, a thin strand of pearly come stretching from his dick to her pussy before draping over Ransom's thigh.

"Yeah, that's right. You're both so good. So damn sexy." Ransom pinched her nipple, drawing her attention back to him. "You up for a rough ride?"

"Always," she panted, though she wasn't sure how much more she could take.

"Levi's going to make sure you admit it if it gets too intense, okay?" Ransom kissed her hard then before saying, "If it does, you tell us. He'll finish me for you."

She nodded, though that wasn't going to happen. They both knew it.

He stood, lifting her and turning her around so that the seat of the stool touched her belly. She had to go onto her tiptoes to reach the floor. Then he laid his hand between her shoulder blades and folded her over it. Ransom kicked her ankles until she spread her legs wide enough to please him.

Then she clung to the chair as he entered her with a single direct thrust that buried him to his balls. A distinctly sexual sound made her sure that Levi's come was overflowing her, making Ransom's pistoning easier.

Levi was there, in front of her, to rub her shoulders as he monitored her reactions.

"She loves your dick as much as I do, Ransom," Levi goaded his friend. "Give it to her, hard and fast. Fuck her so well that she comes when you do."

Rivet wasn't betting on that.

But if she had, she would have been wrong.

Because as Ransom picked up speed and lost himself in her body, she felt herself rising with him. She clung to the stool, even when it tipped onto two legs beneath the force of Ransom's ravishing. And when he wrapped his hand around her hip and found her clit, she realized she was going to fly again.

Levi grinned down at them as he rubbed his own semi-erect cock. "I could do this all damn day. So could Rivet apparently. She's heading there again, Ransom."

"I can feel it." Ransom groaned. "She's so fucking responsive. So perfect. For us."

That thought alone was more arousing to her than anything either of them, or both together, had done to her body. The idea that she might be the gear for their cogs. The person who brought them together and made them functional. That this might be more than the fuck of a lifetime in the kitchen.

Rivet met Levi's stare. She held it as she surrendered, gave herself over to being the spark plug to their engines.

He crouched so he could kiss her as she fell, taking Ransom with her.

Ransom shouted her name, then Levi's as he buried himself as deeply as possible. He held her there, jerking within her as he emptied his balls. He flooded her pussy, his release mingling with Levi's. It felt more right than anything she'd ever experienced.

This was what they'd been made for.

Each other.

And she'd only figured it out in time to lose them if things didn't go well in the coming days.

Even that thought couldn't dull her bliss as she wrung Ransom dry.

It was when he retreated, disconnecting from her body, and gathered her into his arms for a bear hug and Levi joined from the opposite side, that she realized how much more she craved than what they'd already shared.

Rivet wanted everything. Them. As a permanent part of her life.

Unfortunately, she was too scared to even whisper that thought out loud. What if the wheels fell off whatever it was that was forming between them on the true rough ride ahead? What if they didn't, but the guys decided not to stick around anyway after everything was over?

She wasn't sure she could handle being abandoned again.

So for the moment, she pretended like nothing outside their cozy, crappy apartment existed. For the next two days, they had it all.

Too bad it couldn't last.

19

Levi gripped the handlebars so hard, it wouldn't have surprised him if they bent in half.

This was it. They were barreling down the highway with a thunderous roar. Him, Rivet, and Ransom along with another dozen or so of the most seasoned Wildfire members. More were pouring into the site of their confrontation from different directions.

Angus took point, leading their branch of the gang of outlaws like the tip of a spear, aimed straight at the jugular of his enemies. They grew closer and closer to the warehouse where the Savage Skulls were running their illicit operations with every mile that passed beneath their wheels.

And each one of them made him more anxious, more likely to lay his bike down and pretend to take out Ransom and Rivet with him so they couldn't put themselves in harm's way.

The past few days had been heaven. Spending time in their arms, and other parts even more enjoyable on their bodies, he was fully aware of the sacrifices they could be making that night. Worse, he wasn't sure what would happen even if everything went perfectly, which seemed like a long shot.

It terrified him to think of Rivet doing something rash, letting her hatred drown out her common sense, or of Ransom doing something noble to save her, just because the guy thought he deserved to pay more for a split-second decision he'd made as a reckless teenager in a no-win situation.

And Levi...well, he'd gladly trade his life for either of theirs if it came down to it. Maybe then he could show himself, if not them too, that the people he loved most could rely on him to take care of them instead of pushing them into situations where they could be killed.

Either way, they had to get this right. Because none of them was going to make it much longer the way they were going now.

Angus signaled the gang and everyone began to rev their engines, drawing even more attention to themselves as they blasted through the center of the town that housed the Savage Skulls' home base. They weren't capable of subtlety. So instead they went for intimidation.

It seemed to work. There wasn't a soul in sight as they rolled into the lot of the warehouse they'd been tipped off about. Red and Stix were the first off their bikes, busting the lock from the chain and flinging the doors open in seconds.

Levi had barely climbed from his bike, flanking Rivet along with Ransom, who did the same, when someone shouted a curse from inside. There was a tussle, but thankfully no gunshots fired before Red and Stix dragged the president of the Savage Skulls out into the moonlight.

What the fuck? They'd hoped to score more proof of

their rivals' indiscretions or to steal some of their loot as payment for those foul deeds but he hadn't expected they'd get lucky enough to find the president of the Savage Skulls there, unguarded, at this time of night. Levi looked around, wondering how many unfriendly eyes were trained on them from the inky blackness.

Angus cracked his knuckles and approached, planting his boots in the dirt in front of the man. "Good evening, Hector."

"What do you mean by this, Angus?" The man's eyes shifted to the shadows, as if someone would jump out and save him from the wrath of Wildfire. Not likely, Levi thought with a scowl. If his men were nearby, they would be outnumbered and out-armed by Angus's men, who were the baddest of the bad. Why did this asshole have to be so stupid? They weren't going to be able to save him if he didn't do whatever Angus demanded.

And then they'd have another fucking life on their consciences. He hoped the guy rolled over fast so they could get the fuck out of there.

"Motherfucker, you know what I mean." Angus whipped the bag of drugs from inside his leather jacket, slashed it open with the sharp edges of one of his rings, which he'd infamously used to gouge out an enemy's eyes once, then showered his rival with the powder.

"What the fuck!" The guy cursed in Spanish and thrashed, knocking as much of it off of him as possible. "Are you trying to kill me?"

"I should," Angus snarled.

Rivet stood up straighter and Ransom shifted his position so he had a clear line of sight to the interaction. That was because he had insisted on being the one to wear their recording equipment. Right now, if all was working correctly, he was capturing the exchange in both high definition and audio.

All they needed was for Angus to cut some kind of deal with this asshole...or to do something violent. Either way worked, though Levi was hoping for the route with no bloodshed.

Come on, Angus. Say it. Fucking say it. Loud and clear for the camera.

"But if you come to your senses and pay me my cut for running this shit and weapons through my territory, plus a hefty bonus for the stuff you tried to sneak by me already...I might let you live."

FUCK, YES! It took every bit of training Levi had undergone not to scream at the night sky. They had the fucker. That was all they needed to nail him with RICO. Rivet edged closer to Ransom, as if prepared to protect him and the recording he now carried with her life. Levi would do the same.

"Of course, Angus. Of course." Hector knew as well as Levi that Angus would gladly rip his head off instead, then make an even better deal with whoever stepped up to take his place before Hector's body had hit the ground.

"Pops, no!" someone shouted from above them. And when Levi looked up, a shadowy form was perched on the corrugated metal roof of the warehouse, an assault rifle pointed in their direction. Holy fuck, they'd almost gotten away without a scratch. He'd known that was too fucking easy.

"Is that your son?" Angus asked with a sinister smile that fooled no one.

"I'll talk to him. Take all the profit, Angus. Just go. I'll get my house in order and come see you first thing tomorrow," Hector begged, though he had to know it was futile. At this point, Angus wasn't going to leave without reasserting his dominance and demanding respect, not only from Hector but from the rest of the Savage Skulls, who were likely dotting the property around the Wildfire intruders.

Levi huddled closer to Rivet. Between him and Ransom, maybe they could shield her when shit really went down. Which was in three...two...

Angus backhanded Hector, launching his tooth and blood into the dirt. His head lolled and his son lost his shit. Bullets rained down for a moment before Angus reached into his jacket, drew his weapon, and put a bullet between the young man's eyes.

He toppled, falling forward in a slow and nearly graceful layout before his lifeless body hit the ground with a thud, sending up a plume of dust.

Hector howled as if Angus has knocked out the rest of his teeth too.

Angus kicked the man in the ribs, but the rest of the Savage Skulls were too dumb to run. Instead they stood and fought in honor of their fallen comrade and doomed leader. They burst from under tarps and behind fences. Several poured out of the warehouse. Wildfire didn't wait for Angus to give them orders. They dispersed, exchanging gunfire with their rivals.

Fuck that. Levi didn't care who saw. Their only chance now was to stay alive long enough for Jordan and the rest of their backup to arrive and clean up this mess. Their allies were close, but at this point, five minutes would be about as much as he could imagine stalling.

So he grabbed Rivet's hand, then Ransom's, and started running, dragging them after him to the tiny storeroom he'd spotted around the corner of the warehouse.

The three of them fled the war. Ransom kicked down the door with two slams of his tree-trunk leg and they tumbled inside.

What he hadn't counted on was Angus piling in right behind them, then slamming the door.

It was pitch black inside, the only light coming from the pinholes in the roof and the gaps around the eaves of the rickety structure. It took several seconds and some serious blinking before Levi could see anything at all.

But when he did, he realized that Angus had grabbed Rivet and was holding her like a human shield in front of him. Unfortunately, his forearm stretched right across her chest. Which was right about when he realized that Rivet wasn't exactly what she'd always appeared to be.

"What the fuck?" Angus roared. "What is under your shirt?"

Shots rang out around them. If anyone found them, they'd be easier targets than fish in a barrel, and yet...Levi thought it was probably more dangerous in their hiding place than being caught in the crossfire of two rival motorcycle gangs.

Without waiting for a response, Angus whipped open a knife that dropped from up his sleeve and sliced Rivet's hoodie and shirt straight down the center so they hung open. From her grunt, Levi was afraid he'd cut through some of her flesh as well. Shit!

Ransom growled and said, "Angus, enough. It's me you want."

"No!" Levi was not about to let both of his lovers do his fucking job.

"I'm listening, but someone better tell me in the next

two seconds why my newest brother has tits." He flung Rivet to the floor as if she was worthless now that he knew she was a woman.

She hardly hit the ground before she bounced to her feet, facing her nemesis, her hands balled and raised as if she would take him down with her bare hands if she had to. "They don't speak for me."

"She's right." Levi held his hands up. "Rivet and Ransom were just conveniences I found out about along the way. While I was conducting my investigation."

"You're a fucking cop?" Angus's eyes widened and his lips curled. He lifted his dominant hand, which still held his gun, and aimed it at Levi.

Perfect. So long as Angus was focused on him, the bastard couldn't threaten Levi's lovers.

"He might be." Ransom talked over Levi. "But I'm their pawn. I'm the one wearing a wire tonight to try and save my own ass from a lifetime sentence. I told you. It's me you want."

Fuck! Why would he do that? Levi fumed as he thought back to the night Ransom had handed over one of their two bug-sweepers. He should have known the man would out himself, and their evidence, in order to keep from repeating his past sins and either killing someone or getting them killed.

Fuck! Hurry, Jordan! Hurry!

"Don't you dare, Ransom!" Rivet shrieked. "It's not worth it. Let him do whatever he wants to me. Just...get out of here. Take that away from him to someone who can make use of it."

Levi expected Angus to go ballistic.

He didn't. Instead, he got really quiet and narrowed his eyes at Rivet. "Who are you really?"

Fortunately, she was too smart to answer him. Even though he'd murdered her mother, by all accounts he had loved the woman. She'd been his weakness, just like Laurel had been Levi's. And if he was reminded of her betrayal now, he might decide to do the same...or worse... to Rivet.

Cold sweat trickled down Levi's back. He'd only felt this helpless once before in his life, and he'd lived with the repercussions every moment since. Tonight could destroy him. Because if he lost Rivet or Ransom or both... he would never recover.

In that instant he knew the truth. He loved them. More than he'd even loved Laurel, because they knew who he really was and not only accepted him but loved him back.

No, they hadn't said the words, but the bond they shared, the way they were willing to risk everything for each other, told him all he needed to know.

"No, Rivet. Don't!" Ransom shouted over her when she drew a breath to reveal her secrets. He reached into his shirt and ripped the wire off his chest, thrusting it out toward Angus. "Give me your gun and your knife and I'll let you have this. Be smart, Angus."

Wildfire's president didn't hesitate. Any curiosity he had was overridden by his instinct to survive.

He lunged for the recorder.

Ransom let him have it, but in the same motion, he clotheslined Angus, taking him down and sending both his knife and gun skidding away from him. Angus clutched the recorder even as Rivet dove for the gun. When she popped up, she was aiming it right at his head. Levi had no idea how much training she had with firearms. It didn't matter. From this distance, she couldn't miss.

And that's when Ransom shocked them all, maybe Angus most of all, by stepping in between Rivet and their enemy. Levi's heart fell through his stomach.

Whose fucking side was he on?

20

Rivet's heart ripped in her chest. How could Ransom be doing this?

She stared at his big, immovable form standing between her and bringing justice to the murderer who had stolen her mother from her, both when she was alive and when he ordered her death. Even worse, Ransom had betrayed their sacrifices and the work they'd put in by handing Angus the evidence they so desperately needed to make him pay.

If she'd been the one wearing the wire, as she tried to convince him to let her do, she would have gladly let Angus take her out. Jordan would have known to search her body and get what he needed when he arrived, which should be any minute now.

At least she thought so anyway. Time distorted as so many things unfolded at once, not the least of which being Ransom's betrayal. She should have known better than to trust him or Levi. They weren't going to stand by her like they'd promised. And after whatever this was had run its course, they were going to leave her, just like everyone else.

At the moment, she'd be glad to see them go.

Especially Ransom. And for what? Because he was terrified of being responsible for someone's death?

"I went into this knowing what the consequences could be. How dare you do this to us? To me? Why do you get to choose how I end it? Unless you were really working against us the whole time. Is that why you gave him the bug-detector?" Rivet glared at Ransom.

Levi and Angus were silent, for different reasons, she supposed. After all, she was now aiming a gun point blank at Ransom unable to believe this was the same man who'd built her up and made her feel attractive, invincible, and —damn him—loved.

"No, of course not. I'm not doing this to save Angus. Rivet, I'm doing it to save *you*." He looked like he might break down. "Trust me, you will never get over taking someone's life. Even if they're a monster."

Wait, what? He was doing this for her? Because...he *did* care.

"Do you really want to become the exact thing you hate so much? Put down the gun. You're not a murderer, Sevan." Ransom winced. "Not like Angus. Or me."

Oh shit, they were so fucked up. She'd always known that, but now it was going to cost them their lives.

Her thoughts raced as she tried to think of any possible method for circumventing the laws of physics to make her bullet swerve around Ransom and destroy Angus instead.

Angus didn't help himself out any. The bastard chuckled, "Well, thank you, my friend. Whatever your motives are, I appreciate you putting your big ass in front of me."

Rivet's attention snapped to him over Ransom's shoulder, hatred boiling up within her as she finally let him know, as she had so many times before in her mind, exactly why he was going to suffer as soon as she could figure out how to get past Ransom.

She snarled, "Is this how you felt right before you killed my mother?"

Staring at the barrel of her gun, Angus actually fucking laughed. "I probably don't even remember that bitch's name."

"Fuck you." Rivet would have spit on him if she could have. Ransom didn't even give her that satisfaction. Her finger trembled on the trigger of the gun as she prayed Ransom would come to his senses and step aside. "She was your wife, Joanna. I'm here to haunt you for her and send you straight to hell, where you belong."

Angus froze then, squinting at Rivet. He went pale, more afraid of her then than he'd been of storming the Savage Skulls' stronghold. "Joanna? You're her daughter. Her *other* daughter. Joanna. Fuck, she was the love of my life...until she was disloyal. That bitch. Yes, you have her spirit. Her determination and fight. Joanna..."

He trailed off, staring at her with glassy eyes, as if he really had seen a ghost.

Sensing the violent storm brewing with her, Ransom took a step closer and then another until the muzzle of the gun touched his chest. "Give me that, Rivet. Before you do something you regret forever. This might be how your mom would have handled things, but is this you? I don't think so."

He slowly lifted his hand, wrapping it around the pistol and plucking it from her grasp.

Rivet couldn't help it—she wailed. She hadn't even been able to do this one damn thing for her mother and now Angus was going to get away with it all, including ending her life too. Because that's how he operated, kill or be killed. He sure as shit wasn't going to let them walk out of there unscathed simply because he'd thwarted their plans. Or because she carried part of the woman he'd lost.

Distracted, she didn't see Angus move. But Levi did. He screamed, "No!"

The primal terror in his tone made her sure what was about to happen even if she didn't understand how. Angus was about to destroy Ransom, or her. Or all of them.

Except he didn't.

Because Levi charged Angus, throwing himself into the path of the wicked blade the Wildfire president clutched. It must have been sharp as fuck because Levi didn't make a peep when the point buried itself in his flesh instead of Ransom's heart.

He may not have been able to save the person he loved most before, but he did right then. And at what cost?

Angus jerked his hand back, taking the knife with it. He raised it above his head and Ransom rotated, the gun extended in his hand. He hesitated the slightest bit, though she guessed when he weighed Levi's life or his own sanity, she knew which he would pick.

In shock and numb, she stood there, hyperventilating.

They teetered on the brink of catastrophe.

And that's when the door to their sanctuary was ripped open and someone dressed entirely in black pointed a shotgun at them as he bellowed. "Put your hands up. Do not move. This is the FBI. Drop your weapons. Now!"

Rivet followed their instructions, practically a zombie in the aftermath of what had just transpired. The agents bypassed her, Ransom—who set the gun down carefully without discharging it—and Levi, heading straight for Angus. They weren't gentle as they swarmed him, cuffing him then searching him for any additional weapons.

Jordan stepped inside, monitoring his team as they performed their duties with brisk efficiency that made Rivet's head spin. And when he was satisfied, he ordered, "Get him out of here. Don't wait around, transport him to the facility we discussed immediately. I want three men with him twenty-four seven. Go!"

Angus surprised them when he didn't fight. Didn't thrash or attempt to evade Jordan's men. Instead, he turned his head and stared at Rivet every moment until they whisked him from the storage shed. At the last possible moment, he shouted, "I never got over her."

Rivet gave him the finger, completely uncaring about her nudity or her bared breasts, which revealed the woman she'd hidden for so long, then mumbled, "Me either."

Then she collapsed, dropping to her knees on the ground. Ransom joined her and Levi there, yanking them both to him as if he couldn't bear to have even a foot of space between them.

"Are you all okay?" Jordan asked, scanning them each from head to toe.

"We're alive," Ransom responded in a monotone that made her wonder how much more damage his psyche had sustained that evening and if he would be able to heal from it.

"But the recording equipment wasn't as lucky." Rivet gestured at the shattered technology, groaning as her stomach lurched. "Maybe we can piece this back together."

"Nah, it's a goner." Jordan shook his head. "But we don't need it."

"You don't?" Levi rasped, as incredulous as Rivet felt. He picked his head up from where it had lolled against Ransom's shoulder as he practiced deep breathing that was somehow making Rivet feel less panicked too. His hand was clamped over his shoulder and she was pretty sure she was glad she couldn't see clearly enough to realize what damage he was obscuring.

"Nope. Ransom transmitted the whole thing to us live. We weren't sure it was going to work, or that we'd be in range, or that the Savage Skulls wouldn't have some kind of scrambler like Angus does at Wildfire, but we watched that whole shitshow go down from a van parked out on the road." Jordan grinned.

Rivet couldn't believe what she was hearing. He what?

It had been a hell of a risk, but a calculated one. Ransom hadn't betrayed them at all. Of course he hadn't. She should have trusted her heart, but terror and a lifetime of disappointment had kicked in before her rational brain could catch up.

"We all witnessed it," said another guy, who patted Jordan on the back.

"And better yet..." Jordan flipped open an app on his phone and scanned his retina to unlock it. There on the screen they relived every futile second leading up to the moment Angus had destroyed yet another life right in front of them and who knew how many more indirectly. A mother had lost her son. A family had lost a member.

Sure, Hector's son and vice president hadn't been a saint either, but that didn't make it right.

But it would be the last time he fucked someone up as a free man, because it was right there—irrefutable proof of his crimes.

Jordan beamed. "He's going away for life. It probably would have been kinder if you'd let Rivet kill him."

"For Angus, sure. Prison sucks. But not for her." Ransom nodded solemnly. "And she's the one I love."

Ransom had condemned Angus to take his place, locked up for life.

He also surprised the shit out of her. "You *love* me?"

"Um, shit. Guys. Not to ruin the moment, but do you think someone could sew me up quick?" Levi groaned and swayed, his hand squeezing his shoulder.

Both Ransom and Rivet abandoned their conversation and focused on their partner. As one of the agents shone a light on Levi's wound, the blood pouring between his fingers made her realize that his black leather vest had been hiding an injury far worse than she'd realized.

And that's when Jordan's people swooped in, taking him, Ransom, and Rivet into custody and separating them to administer first aid, help them recover, and begin the interrogation and witness statement process.

Rivet had lots to say, but not to Jordan and his team. She was dying to talk to Ransom, and Levi.

Had her fear and doubts ruined any shot at a future with either or both of them?

Sure, they'd lived, but would they still be able to be whole as individuals or something more after everything that had happened that night?

21

Rivet sat at the steel table, her arms folded on top of it and her head resting on them. Exhaustion made her bleary. Half-awake, half-dead, she wasn't sure what she was anymore. Mostly she was sick at the thought of the position she'd put Ransom in, how close they had been to a deadly mistake, and how Levi had gotten injured because of it.

She had nearly fucked everything up at the critical moment and only had them to thank for salvaging the operation.

As she sat there, finally left alone by the agents and who-knew-who-else who'd questioned her about Angus's operations relentlessly for hours, all she could think of was how scared she'd been. Not of Angus, or even of dying, but of believing her gut might be right for once. That Ransom could care for her. Okay, fuck it...that he might *love* her enough to protect her from herself. And that Levi could have the same feelings for her as he did for Ransom. After all, he'd risked his life for them both...

Damn, she'd fucked up.

Despite their actions and Ransom's declaration about how he'd felt before the botched takedown, Rivet had no reason to expect that they'd be willing to forgive her or give her another chance to prove that she believed in them as much as they'd believed in her.

She had no idea how long they left her there, stewing in her own misery, before the door opened again. It took all the energy she had left to blink her eyes and see who was going to bug her next. When she did, she realized it was a familiar face staring at her in concern.

Jordan opened the door, then stepped aside so that Joy could join them.

Joy!

"Sevan!" her sister squealed before darting to her side and hugging her tight. It seemed odd to hear her real name after so long. It reminded her of how Ransom had used it to get through to her when everything had been burning down around them. "Are you okay? You look wretched. Is everyone all right?"

"I—I don't know." Rivet looked to Jordan, hoping for clarification.

No one had given her an update on Levi's condition, and Ransom's mental state would be even harder to diagnose by someone who didn't know him as well as she did.

"They made it through." He was in operative mode, so different from the man she'd heard about from her sister, who knew him best as part of the Hot Rides family and the doting boyfriend of his two lovers. "Ransom and Levi are ready to go too if you wouldn't mind taking the three of them to Hot Rides. As key witnesses, we'll need them to stay close in case there are any other questions, and also so the guys can help us watch their backs for a while. But I figured you could use some time to yourselves to work through everything that's happened."

Jordan cleared his throat. While he didn't mention it in front of her sister, he was aware that the three of them had developed a relationship. She'd divulged that fact at some point during the endless night as if it hadn't been obvious from the way they'd looked at each other during the raid and her concern for them in the aftermath.

"Okay, then, let's get out of here." Joy helped Rivet stand and held on to her until her legs stopped wobbling.

"Ransom and Levi should be in the lobby by the time you get there." Jordan smiled at Rivet. "Good luck with them."

She would need it. "Uh, yeah. Thanks. You're okay with them coming too?"

"Up to you," Joy said.

"One extra person in your place would be a lot. Where would three of us stay?" Rivet asked, then turned to Jordan. "Maybe I'll go with Joy, and Ransom and Levi could bunk at the mountain house?"

It was a presumptuous ask, but she couldn't stand to make things awkward if they didn't want anything to do with her.

Jordan surprised her by breaking into a chuckle. "They—and you, of course—are always welcome. But I don't think they'd accept my invitation even if I offered. They've been badgering me about you nonstop. Besides, Joy has a surprise for you that you might want to share with them."

"You do?" Rivet whipped her stare to Joy. But her brain was still processing what Jordan had said. Ransom and Levi still gave a shit about her? Maybe she hadn't ruined everything after all.

"Um, yeah. I'd rather show you than tell you about it, though." Joy beamed. "Come on."

She squeezed Rivet's hand and led her from the room, down the hall, and to the lobby, where her gaze was instantly drawn to Levi. He paced in front of Ransom, who was slumped in an uncomfortable-looking chair. The moment he looked up and locked stares with her, he froze. Ransom noticed and lifted his head until he too was focused entirely on her.

What was she supposed to do?

"Go to them." Joy poked her in the small of her back. Hard.

So she went. Except she didn't walk. Rivet ran and flung herself at Levi, trusting that he would be there to catch her, and if not, that Ransom would grab them both. She might fall flat on her face or...

She might end up in his embrace.

Which was exactly what happened.

He grunted as he hugged her with his good arm, squeezing her tight. Then he dipped his head and kissed her right there in front of their friends, her sister, and Ransom. Even the other agents, case be damned. He must have come clean with Jordan and his team since he wasn't trying to hide their connection anymore, so hell if she would either.

"How are you?" she asked, running her hands over the bandage she could see peeking out from beneath the sleeve of his borrowed T-shirt.

"Perfect now that both of you are with me again." He looked over his shoulder at Ransom and jerked his chin toward the door. "Can we get out of here?"

"Yeah," Joy answered him. "I'm your ride."

Ransom didn't budge. "I'm all right, thanks."

Rivet's heart dropped. He hadn't forgiven her for doubting him, and she didn't blame him either. She prepared to walk out of there without him. If Levi decided to stay by his side, where she was no longer welcome, she would understand.

Levi, however, wasn't having any of that. "Where will you go, Ransom?"

He shrugged.

Joy interjected, "Please. This isn't the place to settle these things. Come with me. With us. I think I have a solution for you."

"I doubt that," Ransom mumbled, but he stood.

Rivet shot her sister a huge, grateful smile.

Jordan wandered from the interrogation rooms, shaking his head at them. He addressed Levi and Ransom, "Guys, I know things might be weird now that the investigation is wrapped and real life is slapping you in the face, but try to keep an open mind. And stick around in case we need to talk some more. Please. I promise you it will be worth it."

Was he talking about more than their professional arrangements?

"So you're really gonna let me walk out of here?" Ransom asked, one brow raised. He wrung his hands as he eyed the door.

"Yeah. You're a free man. And a damn good one too." Jordan clapped Ransom on the shoulder. "Thank you for everything you did here. The three of you. You've made a real difference, not only to me."

"Yo, Jordan!" A super-hot man wearing black cargo pants jerked his thumb over his shoulder. "You're going to want to hear this."

Whatever it was, Rivet was glad not to be involved. She

wondered how many other guys Jordan had working for him in his unofficial capacity and what other things they might get up to. Then again, she was ready to return to living a simple, boring life.

If she could find a way to snag these two hot men of her own, she'd consider that plenty enough excitement for one woman to handle.

As if by some tacit understanding, the three of them were quiet as Joy led them to her car and they piled inside. The guys insisted she take the front seat while they sat squished in the back on either side of Arden's baby seat. Rivet might have laughed had things not been so tense.

Joy reached over and squeezed Rivet's hand while she drove. Each of them was lost in their own thoughts until they turned into the Hot Rides driveway. Up ahead, Rivet spied a giant blob of balloons and a banner hanging on a tiny home she would have sworn hadn't been there when she'd briefly visited before getting sucked back into the inferno.

"What's all this?" Levi asked as he peered through the windshield.

Rivet would have answered, but she was already getting choked up as she could make out the words on the sign, which looked hand-painted. It said *Welcome home!*

Joy parked and turned in her seat to look at Rivet. "I hope you know this is your place, if you want it. We would love to have you—all three of you—here, with us for the long haul. So, while you were gone, we sort of..."

"You built your sister a house?" Ransom asked in disbelief.

"It's, you know, small but it has all the essentials." Joy sniffled. "It's right next to mine, Dane, and Walker's. I know Arden would love having her aunt around as she grows up. And so would I. Please, don't go now that I've just found you."

Rivet was floored. Tears rolled down her cheeks as the house and sign and the promise of everything she'd ever desired materialized right there in front of her, within reach.

And now that she had it, she could only imagine how empty it would be, without someone—*two someones*—to share it with.

"Joy, that's..." Rivet lunged across the center console and tackled her sister. "Thank you."

Joy practically smothered her, she hugged her so hard. Then, with both of them wiping their eyes on their shirts like mirror images of each other, they started laughing. "Everyone's waiting over there. Let's tell them the good news."

The four of them climbed from the car, Ransom's knees cracking as he unfolded his big frame.

"I feel like I'm intruding." He looked over his shoulder, but there was only miles of woods and empty road, nowhere to go but forward.

"You're not," Rivet and Joy said in unison.

Quinn came out to meet them. As the shop manager and the unofficial head of the Hot Rides gang, his endorsement went a long way. "So glad to see you home, Sevan. And you guys too. I apologize in advance. My friends are dying to meet you and, you know, we take any excuse to have some of Devra's cooking, so she made a bunch of food for us. The spread is over at the garage in the break room, if you're ready to celebrate with us. If that's too much right now, we understand and it will keep. But I wanted to officially tell you that we're excited you might be joining us in the shop and in our lives. You're welcome here. All three of you."

Rivet would have flung herself at him like she had at her sister if Levi hadn't beat her to it. She knew it was every bit as important to him to find a place where he could be accepted as himself. For him, Hot Rides would be a welcome oasis.

"Thank you. Seriously. You have no idea what that means to me," Levi admitted as Quinn hugged him back. Then he retreated, coming to stand by her side.

Ransom seemed less certain but every bit as grateful. "That's a really generous offer. I'm just not sure..."

Joy bit her lip as she looked between Levi, Rivet, and Ransom. Rivet wished she could say she felt more confident than her sister looked that the three of them could pull it together. But she vowed right then that she was going to give it her best shot.

Because these people—all of the Hot Rides, plus their friends the Hot Rods gang and the Powertools crew—had already shown her what was possible and how good it could be if they pulled it off.

It was worth risking rejection and getting her heart crushed.

So she drew a deep breath, then turned to Levi and Ransom.

"Maybe we could go for a walk in the woods and talk about this in private?" Rivet asked. If they said no, if they bailed, she'd only have herself to blame this time.

Except they didn't.

They stuck, at least long enough to hear her out.

"We can do that," Levi held out his hand to her, entwining their fingers. He looked to his best friend, pleading really. "Will you come with us, Ransom?"

Rivet extended her hand to him and held her breath. She didn't have to wait long for Ransom to engulf hers with his own and nod.

Together, they set off into the woods, and she could only hope they didn't lose their way.

22

Levi took his first deep breath in over twenty-four hours, drawing fresh air into his lungs. It was an unseasonably warm day, the temperature reaching into the low eighties. Everything was green, new leaves budded and unfurled, and crystal clear water trickled through the stream meandering beside the path.

It felt like he'd either fallen down the rabbit hole or been reborn into a new world where the purpose of the past two years had vanished. In its place, he had something even more dangerous. Hope.

So long as the man and woman he loved could work out whatever had slid sideways between them, he might have a chance to salvage the relationship they'd been building before everything had gone to hell. And suddenly, that's what he wanted more than anything.

Because the reality was, he'd already opened his heart to them. The risk now was whether or not he could hold on to them or if he was doomed to lose one or both like he'd already lost Laurel. That would hurt, almost worse, because they knew him and accepted him fully.

He drew in another breath, filling his lungs to capacity in an effort to stretch out the crushing pressure in his chest at that thought.

"Do you hear that?" Rivet asked, tipping her face up into the mottled sunlight that filtered through the early spring leaves.

Levi canted his head and strained, but he didn't notice a damn thing. "No. What?"

"Nothing. Absolutely nothing." A huge smile crossed her face, making her even more beautiful than usual. "No bikers shouting at me. No gunshots. No clubhouse music. Nothing. Isn't it great?"

"It is." He smiled at her as he led them to a mossy embankment, then tugged them to a stop. They were plenty far enough away from the shop to guarantee their privacy.

"I could get used to this," Ransom agreed, his eyes unfocused as he stared into the endless emerald ocean surrounding them.

"Then why don't you?" Rivet asked quietly. "You heard Joy. They built a place for me here. And my place is your place. If you'll accept it. Levi's too, of course."

"I don't belong with you." He shook his head, dropping Rivet's hand.

"Why not?" she wondered.

Levi clenched his teeth as he prepared for what was about to come. He hoped that, like venom from a snakebite, they could express their poisonous pasts and recover instead of letting their wounds fester and destroy them both. For their sakes, but also his own.

"I saw the fear in your eyes, Sevan. When it came down to it, you rightly believed I was the terrible human being I am and that I could even think about lifting a finger to hurt you." He hugged himself as if that had hurt him more than Angus's knife had injured Levi's shoulder, which still stung like a bitch.

"I'm sorry." Rivet bridged the gap between them and looped her arms around his waist. "Craig, that was not a reflection on you. It was all about me and my twisted beliefs. I was freaking out and my instincts went to that place, the one I spent my nights in as a little girl, where my mom had left me for Angus. Where she showed me that love isn't guaranteed or as strong as you might like it to be."

Levi stepped closer to them both, putting a hand on each of their backs. "You mashed each other's buttons. Not on purpose, but in the heat of that incredibly stressful moment, all of our history was working against us, mine included. That was the worst of us. And we survived it. Why don't we focus on the best of us instead, and promise to try to get even better? Together."

"Is that really what you want?" Rivet asked, her gorgeous eyes peering up from beneath her thick lashes. He wondered if she intended to go back to her feminine style or if she'd gotten used to being Rivet. Either way, he adored her.

He nodded. "Yeah."

"And you?" Rivet asked Ransom. "Do you believe me?"

He didn't answer right way, really thinking about it.

"I'm so sorry, Ransom. I didn't mean to let my insecurities hurt you." She turned away, probably so they wouldn't see her when she broke down.

"Ah, fuck." He growled as he wrapped his arms around her from behind then rocked her. "Don't cry, Sevan. I'm not worth your tears, but I believe you anyway. Your heart is too big to be good for you. You might be wrong, but you don't think anywhere as badly of me as I think of myself."

Rivet spun in his hold and threw her arms around his neck, practically climbing him so she could mesh their mouths. Levi probably should have been jealous, but instead he was relieved and...frankly...turned on. He cupped his burgeoning erection through his jeans.

The adrenaline of the past day could use an outlet.

Woods or no woods, he wasn't leaving this spot until they'd bonded again, so neither of his lovers could deny that they belonged together. Besides, there was something he needed from them too. So while they made out, he shucked his jeans then his shirt. It took him an extra few seconds due to the stiffness in his arm, but he managed.

"What the hell are you doing?" Rivet asked, breathless as she and Ransom tried to suck in a few lungfuls of air, still nibbling on each other's lips in between them.

"I'm going to remind you both how well we go together, fucked up or not. This is us. This is who we are —somehow I've found the perfect pair of partners to fit me. I'm going to prove it to you, too."

Rivet squirmed until Ransom put her down. She grinned up at Levi, then shrugged. "Sounds good to me."

She whipped off the too-big loaner shirt one of the cops had given her, her breasts bare and unbound beneath it. The long, angry scratch between them reminded him that none of them had escaped Angus unscathed. They'd all probably have scars from that night.

But that didn't mean they couldn't try to heal each other.

"Ah, shit. Rivet." He reached for her, taking them down to the surprisingly comfortable mossy ground so that he could kiss every inch of the line.

While he did, he was glad to see that Ransom didn't balk. The man stripped and joined him in no time, repeating Levi's kisses all over again.

They would be even stronger, as long as they stayed together.

Rivet reached for Ransom and said, "I want you inside me. Please. Use me to make yourself feel better. I hate seeing that desolate look in your eyes and knowing that I put it there."

"You didn't," he promised. "I did. I can't believe that you still want me even after everything."

"I don't want you." She rushed on so he didn't get the wrong idea. "I *need* you."

He nodded once then dropped lower, his gorgeous body covering her completely. Ransom jerked himself a few times, pumping up his already mostly hard cock. So Levi joined them, lying beside them for a better look.

They had taken hardly any time to prepare, so he ran his hand down Rivet's body to make sure she would be able to accept Ransom as easily as possible. He ran his fingers along her slit, surprised to find her already wet.

Ransom growled when he saw her slickness glistening on her folds and Levi's fingers. So Levi brought his hand to his mouth and licked the taste of her from them. His cock practically drilled into her hip as he rocked involuntarily when Ransom began to work his cock into her.

Tendons in his neck stood out as he tried to restrain himself, but he shouldn't have bothered. Rivet grasped his shoulders and pulled, tugging him closer. She cried out when Ransom sank into her with one steady, unrelenting plunge.

"You like how that looks, when I'm buried in her?"

Ransom asked Levi, who nodded enthusiastically. "Good. Because you're next."

Ransom leaned over and kissed Levi with more intention and passion than he could recall experiencing before. He thrust his tongue between Levi's lips even as he did the same with his cock, fucking Rivet.

It wasn't subtle or romantic or sweet, but it was everything else—fierce, possessive, and a little desperate. He was claiming them both, and Levi wasn't about to argue.

In fact, he wished Ransom would do the same to him, though he figured he'd have to wait for round two later on to make that dream a reality.

Ransom tore his mouth from Levi's so he could drive more powerfully into Rivet, hunching over to really dig in, and at the same time he bit her nipple.

Levi helped out by cupping her other breast and teasing it while Ransom did his thing. Rivet stared up at him, her mouth frozen in a shocked O as they ravished her together.

It didn't take long before her heels drummed on the moss and she was shuddering beneath Ransom. She arched then bucked, coming all over his best friend's cock as she screamed his name, startling a couple of birds nearby into flight.

Levi was shocked when Ransom didn't come with her. Instead he withdrew, his cock soaked with her natural lubrication, then commanded Levi, "Go ahead. Take my place."

"I can wait." Levi didn't intend to force Rivet to take him simply because he hadn't had a turn.

"No, you can't." She grabbed him by the dick, kind of turning him on more, then led him between her legs.

Ransom took the opportunity to dip his index and middle fingers into her pussy, which still clenched periodically.

Rivet groaned and her hips rocked up to meet him. She really did need more.

So Levi didn't hesitate. He put his cock beside Ransom's fingers and pushed inside her, groaning as her heat and slickness welcomed him. Ransom let him take over, withdrawing his hand with one last caress along Levi's length.

He was so engrossed in fusing them completely that it surprised him when Ransom slipped the same hand between Levi's ass cheeks. And it caught him even more off guard when the man probed his hole with his wet fingers.

"Oh fuck, yes." Being filled while fucking Rivet was one of his deepest, darkest fantasies. Something he'd imagined a million times but never imagined could happen.

And now it was about to.

Rivet smiled up at him. "What's he doing back there?"

"Using his fingers to fuck me." Levi pounded into her without the finesse he wished he possessed right then. She didn't seem to mind, hugging him tight, careful not to disturb his wound while caressing every other part of him she could reach.

"Would you like it better if it was his cock instead?" Rivet asked. "He was so fucking big and hard inside me. I bet that would feel so good if he put it in your ass. Wouldn't it?"

Levi froze, afraid he might shoot at the thought alone. "Yes." He looked over his shoulder at Ransom. "Do that. Please. Do that."

"We don't have any lube." Ransom frowned.

"I saw how she came all over you. Just do it." Levi grunted as he buried himself to the balls in Rivet. He was so high on her that he wouldn't feel any pain. And truth be told, he might get off on it if he did.

"Give him what he asked for," Rivet coached Ransom. "He has a right to decide for himself. And he needs to know you want him. Like this. With me."

"You know I think it's hot when you bend over for me." Ransom came closer, murmuring in Levi's ear as Levi continued to fuck Rivet, though with shorter, jerkier strokes now that both of his lovers were conspiring to make him unravel. "Don't you?"

Levi thought so, but he was man enough to admit it relieved him to hear it. Both Rivet and Ransom accepted him. They treasured him. Exactly how he was and no matter who he craved.

"Show me," Levi begged. "Fuck me."

Ransom didn't make him ask again. He cursed as he fit himself to Levi's body and pressed the barest bit inside. It burned, he wasn't going to lie, but the lubrication Rivet had provided for him made it possible for Ransom to find his way home.

Ransom was gentle but insistent as he drilled deeper and deeper.

And when he hesitated to make sure Levi was okay, Levi pulled almost all the way out of Rivet, impaling himself on Ransom's fat cock. Fuck, it felt so good he could cry.

When Rivet used her thumb to brush away his tears, he realized he actually was.

"Does it hurt?" she whispered.

"No, it's fixing the hurt. Taking it away. This is what I've needed for so long, even when I didn't understand it myself. You are what I need. Both of you." Levi kissed her then, letting himself get lost in her touches, her body holding him tight even as Ransom filled him beyond belief.

They made love in the dappled sunlight, their moans, cries, and grunts drowning out everything else in the world that wasn't about pleasure, love, and worshipping each other.

He wasn't sure how long they kept it up, but eventually Rivet's pussy began to clamp tighter on him, and Ransom's hands, which gripped his hips as he plowed into Levi's ass, mimicked the pressure on his dick.

Levi let them have him. All of him. He would never in his life forget the way it felt to be surrounded by their adoration and approval. He should have warned Ransom that he was close, but he couldn't gather his thoughts into coherent sentences.

So instead he showed them what they did to him. He lifted his head, stared straight into Rivet's eyes and roared as he came. His ass clenched on Ransom's shaft as he unloaded into Rivet's soft, sweet pussy. He overflowed her with jet after jet of his release.

Which seemed to trigger her own climax.

She gazed back at him and Ransom smiled, then let go. Rivet flew, coming around him, milking the last of his come from his balls.

Ransom couldn't resist the show they put on for him or the effects of Levi's body, massaging his cock. He shouted their names, then paused before erupting into a flurry of motion. Hot spurts of his seed flooded Levi's ass, causing aftershocks to race through his body.

He'd never come so hard in his life.

For a while, he floated, probably squashing Rivet as he

collapsed on top of her. If so, she didn't seem to mind, crooning how well he'd fucked her and how much she loved watching him come apart. She and Ransom hugged him, sneaking caresses of each other in between their gentle petting.

"You still alive?" Rivet eventually asked with a sexy laugh.

"I might be in heaven, not sure." Levi chuckled too then, because it sounded like some kind of cheesy line, even though he meant every word. He tried to be more serious, so they would understand how much what they'd shared mattered to him. He figured the best way to do that was just to blurt, "I love you. Both of you."

Rivet squeezed him and Ransom did too.

"We love you too," Ransom promised, and Rivet nodded, her eyes going glassy with more tears.

Ransom rolled to his feet and held his hand out to Levi, who took it. Then they each extended one to Rivet to lift her up too. She rose, dusting moss particles from her ass and arms.

As if she was uncomfortable with how intense their conversation had gotten, she joked around with them as they hastily got dressed, reminding Levi of how much he enjoyed both of his best friends' company, even when they weren't fooling around.

"Do you think we'll ever have sex in a bed?" Rivet groused.

"Overrated." Levi grinned. "Besides I don't care where we are, as long as I have you both."

"Technically, the two of you did fuck in a bed once. That time in the motel..." Ransom winked.

"That doesn't count." Rivet shook her head. "I mean a nice, clean bed that doesn't squeak every time you breathe. I know where we can find one of those, thanks to my sister and the rest of the Hot Rides, Hot Rods, and Powertools. Can you believe they did that for us?"

"They did it for you," Levi reminded her. "Because Joy does love you, and I am pretty fucking sure that she—like us—will never take you for granted like your mother did. Okay?"

She froze, then looked up at him. "Do you mean that?"

"That I don't plan to make the same mistakes again? That I adore you and will cherish your love every moment of every day for the rest of my life? That I will give you... and Ransom...my own heart? Um, yup. All of that."

Rivet beamed. She glanced at Ransom as if to see if he was as surprised as she was.

He shrugged. "I guess there's no point in denying it. You two are everything to me. You saved me, even if it was from myself. And I'll never forget that or let you deal with your issues on your own again. I'll be here, every day, to remind you how much I love you and want the best for you, even when you don't think you deserve it."

A tear slipped out of the corner of Rivet's eye, but she smiled instead of sobbing. "I love you too. Both of you. And nothing would make me happier than if you would agree to move in with me so we can figure out the future, together."

"Not even sex in that nice, clean bed of yours?" Levi teased.

She laughed. "Bed of *ours*, you mean."

"Yeah." He liked the sound of that.

"Well, that would be pretty awesome too. Let's go home and try it out," Rivet suggested.

When the guys didn't move fast enough to suit her, too busy grinning at each other, she jogged away from them before shouting over her shoulder, "First one there can show me what Levi likes so much about anal sex..."

Levi shoved Ransom, sticking his foot out to trip him, not afraid to play dirty.

He laughed as he tore through the woods, spring air filling his lungs even as the sound of Sevan and Craig's laughter spurred him to run faster, straight into their bed and their future.

23

J oe stood at the window of Gavyn's house, staring wistfully down the curved driveway that led to the Hot Rides shop, the tiny homes he'd built with the rest of his Powertools crew, and the woods beyond. Aside from Levi and Ransom chasing Rivet, who squealed and laughed, toward their newly completely house, it should have been peaceful, and yet... restlessness clawed at him.

His uncle Tom came up behind him and rested his hand on Joe's shoulder, the slightly gnarled and bonier fingers still strong as fuck where they gripped him. "What're you thinking about?"

He considered evading the question, but Tom would know. He always did.

So Joe saved them both some time and turned around to face not only his uncle but also his cousin, Eli—who owned the Hot Rods car restoration business down the road—and Quinn, the manager of Hot Rides. The guys had quit joking around and glanced over periodically as if they weren't secretly paying rapt attention to his conversation with Tom.

"Thinking about how much I miss the rest of the crew." Joe sighed and wandered over to the couch, plopping down beside Eli, who might as well have been his brother instead of his cousin. They'd been though some shit together, including the death of Eli's mother when they were kids.

"You're heading back tomorrow morning," Quinn laughed. "I'm sure they'll welcome you home crew-style to make up for your extra time apart, no worries."

"I didn't say I was horny, dumbass." Joe's mouth twisted as if he'd bitten into something sour, because he was that too. "I said I miss them and…"

Tom sat on his other side and angled inward, refusing to let Joe off the hook now that he'd unearthed the doubts that had been nagging him for months.

"And?" his uncle prodded.

"I'm wondering how much worse it would be if Morgan, me, and the kids moved here." There, he'd said it. And it felt so fucking good to put the idea out there in the room and in the universe.

He'd obviously surprised them since for once in their lives they were absolutely silent.

At least for a few moments.

"Whoa." Quinn leaned forward in the chair opposite them, putting his elbows on his knees. "Are you seriously considering that?"

"You know we'd fucking love to have you closer to us." Eli turned toward Joe, his face cautiously optimistic and yet concerned. The man would always have his back, and that meant doing what was best for Joe and his family, even if it wasn't always best for Eli himself.

"I guess it's just that as I get older, I realize how important family is." Joe crashed into the back of the couch, covering his face with his hands. "But what do you do when you have two branches of your family and they're not in the same place?"

"You've been doing your best, coming out here so often this past year," Tom said quietly.

"I know. But every trip only makes me wish we didn't have to leave again." Joe's heart pounded now that he was voicing these things that had been eating at him for a while. "I fucking love my wife, and our kids, and the rest of the Powertools crew. Our business rocks. I have just about everything I've always dreamed of and things I didn't even know were possible. What right do I have to be discontent?"

"It's brave of you to admit to yourself that you are." Tom squeezed his knee. "Life is a long road, Joe. You never reach the end of it until the day you die. Things change. People change. And that's okay. I don't know what the right answer is—only you and Morgan and the rest of the crew can say. But I am sure that you're strong enough to figure it out together."

Quinn nodded. "It's because of you guys that I have what I do today. You showed me what to strive for and I admire you for refusing to settle, even if what you have is pretty damn good already."

It was hard to imagine Barracuda's little bro was grown enough to be married to his best friend and his best friend's wife, but here he was giving Joe advice. Solid guidance that was making a lot of sense to him right then.

That was a trip.

It also made it obvious that what they were telling him was true. Things changed. People grew up and matured.

Quinn wasn't a kid anymore, making dumb mistakes or running from his past. Joe owed it to his wife, and their friends—who were also sometimes lovers—to be honest about his recent unrest. Otherwise, this feeling would fester and ruin what he had anyway.

Then where would he be?

Still, it wasn't going to be easy. Nah, it wasn't even conceivable, which was why he'd been spinning his tires since last summer.

"Mike is my best fucking friend. My wife loves the rest of the crew and their wives and kids as much as I do. And she's got the bakery to worry about." Joe shook his head. "It's impossible. I should just forget it…"

"You know…" Quinn added with a smirk. "Last time you guys all came out in the party bus, for the New Year's Eve thing, I heard Devra and Morgan trading recipes and Devra wishing that Morgan was closer so she could supply the restaurant."

Joe's heart fucking stuttered in his chest. "You're lying."

"Nope." Quinn held his hands up, palms out. "Ask your wife."

"Maybe I will." But probably not, because the thought of uprooting their lives was exhausting and terrifying even if some kernel of his soul knew it would make him complete.

"I hope you do," Tom said before ruffling Joe's hair. "You know you always were Michelle's favorite."

"Hey!" Eli shoved Joe's shoulder, making him knock into Tom. "What about me?"

"Her favorite *nephew*. You were, of course, her favorite son."

"I was her only goddamn son." Eli pouted pretty hard for a grown ass man with a husband and wife of his own.

How had they gotten so damn lucky? Joe was grateful, he was. But that didn't mean he shouldn't try to give his family the best of everything he could manage.

What would the crew say if he told them what he had in mind now? Would they support him like they always had—even when he'd first suggested that they fool around together—or this time was he dreaming too big?

Joe was afraid to hope, but also scared of doing nothing and regretting it for the rest of his life.

"So you're going to talk to them when you get home, right?" Tom prodded.

"I'm going to try Morgan first and see what she thinks." Joe sighed. If nothing else, his wife would always be honest and supportive. Through the ups and downs, she'd always been there, even when he hadn't been able to give her the things she desired most, like a child. Well, they'd found a way, but it hadn't been conventional or without stress. Hell, it had nearly ripped them apart.

And that was what he was afraid of.

Would she move to Middletown with him even if it meant sacrificing their friends and their home, simply because it made him happy?

Probably.

Would she be satisfied with him alone after being spoiled by the rest of the crew—in bed and out—for so long?

Probably not.

So he'd have to think carefully about how to explain his yearning so they could decide what was best for them and their family, both the one they'd chosen and the one they were born into.

Life was funny sometimes. Just when you thought you

had it figured the fuck out, some new wrinkle would present itself and test you all over again.

Well, he was ready to fight for the happiest future they could build for each other.

"No matter what happens, Joe, we're here for you," Tom promised. "Powertools, Hot Rods, and Hot Rides...we stick together."

And that's exactly what he was afraid of. Would he be breaking their unspoken pact if he left the crew behind, for good? Or were Powertools really for life?

They were about to find out.

THAT'S RIGHT, the original Powertools crew are coming back for another round of steamy stories!

Preorder the first book in the continuing Powertools universe series HERE. It will, of course include updates on all your favorite Hot Rods and Hot Rides characters as well.

Thank you for loving this world as much as I do!

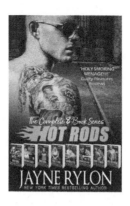

If you missed out on the Powertools: Hot Rods series, you can buy all eight books in a discounted single-volume boxset by clicking HERE.

If you'd like to start at the very beginning with the Powertools Crew, you can download a discounted boxset of the first six books HERE.

Yes, know it says complete series but I wrote a seventh book more recently and haven't gotten around to updating the boxset yet, sorry!

You can find the seventh Powertools book, More the Merrier, HERE.

CLAIM A $5 GIFT CERTIFICATE

Jayne is so sure you will love her books, she'd like you to try any one of your choosing for free. Claim your $5 gift certificate by signing up for her newsletter. You'll also learn about freebies, new releases, extras, appearances, and more!

www.jaynerylon.com/newsletter

WHAT WAS YOUR FAVORITE PART?

Did you enjoy this book? If so, please leave a review and tell your friends about it. Word of mouth and online reviews are immensely helpful and greatly appreciated.

JAYNE'S SHOP

Check out Jayne's online shop for autographed print books, direct download ebooks, reading-themed apparel up to size 5XL, mugs, tote bags, notebooks, Mr. Rylon's wood (you'll have to see it for yourself!) and more.
www.jaynerylon.com/shop

LISTEN UP!

The majority of Jayne's books are also available in audio format on Audible, Amazon and iTunes.

ABOUT THE AUTHOR

 Jayne Rylon is a *New York Times* and *USA Today* bestselling author who has sold more than one million books. She has received numerous industry awards including the Romantic Times Reviewers' Choice Award for Best Indie Erotic Romance and the Swirl Award, which recognizes excellence in diverse romance. She is an Honor Roll member of the Romance Writers of America. Her stories used to begin as daydreams in seemingly endless business meetings, but now she is a full time author, who employs the skills she learned from her straight-laced corporate existence in the business of writing. She lives in Ohio with her husband, the infamous Mr. Rylon, and their cat, Frodo. When she can escape her purple office, she loves to travel the world, avoid speeding tickets in her beloved Sky, SCUBA dive, hunt Pokemon, and–of course–read.

Jayne Loves To Hear From Readers
www.jaynerylon.com
contact@jaynerylon.com
PO Box 10, Pickerington, OH 43147

facebook.com/jaynerylon

twitter.com/JayneRylon

instagram.com/jaynerylon

youtube.com/jaynerylonbooks

bookbub.com/profile/jayne-rylon

amazon.com/author/jaynerylon

ALSO BY JAYNE RYLON

4-EVER

A New Adult Reverse Harem Series

4-Ever Theirs

4-Ever Mine

EVER AFTER DUET

Reverse Harem Featuring Characters From The 4-Ever Series

Fourplay

Fourkeeps

EVER & ALWAYS DUET

Reverse Harem Featuring Characters from the 4-Ever and Ever After Duets

Four Money

Four Love

POWERTOOLS: THE ORIGINAL CREW

Five Guys Who Get It On With Each Other & One Girl. Enough Said?

Kate's Crew

Morgan's Surprise

Kayla's Gift

Devon's Pair

Nailed to the Wall

Hammer it Home

More the Merrier *NEW*

POWERTOOLS: HOT RODS

Powertools Spin Off. Keep up with the Crew plus...

Seven Guys & One Girl. Enough Said?

King Cobra

Mustang Sally

Super Nova

Rebel on the Run

Swinger Style

Barracuda's Heart

Touch of Amber

Long Time Coming

POWERTOOLS: HOT RIDES

Powertools and Hot Rods Spin Off.

Menage and Motorcycles

Wild Ride

Slow Ride

Hard Ride

Joy Ride

Rough Ride

POWERTOOLS: RETURN OF THE CREW

The original crew is back with more steamy polyamorous stories!

Screwed

Drilled

Grind

Pound

MEN IN BLUE

Hot Cops Save Women In Danger

Night is Darkest

Razor's Edge

Mistress's Master

Spread Your Wings

Wounded Hearts

Bound For You

DIVEMASTERS

Sexy SCUBA Instructors By Day, Doms On A Mega-Yacht By Night

Going Down

Going Deep

Going Hard

STANDALONE

Menage

Middleman

Nice & Naughty

Contemporary

Where There's Smoke

Report For Booty

COMPASS BROTHERS

Modern Western Family Drama Plus Lots Of Steamy Sex

Northern Exposure

Southern Comfort

Eastern Ambitions

Western Ties

COMPASS GIRLS

Daughters Of The Compass Brothers Drive Their Dads Crazy And Fall In Love

Winter's Thaw

Hope Springs

Summer Fling

Falling Softly

COMPASS BOYS

Sons Of The Compass Brothers Fall In Love

Heaven on Earth

Into the Fire

Still Waters

Light as Air

PLAY DOCTOR

Naughty Sexual Psychology Experiments Anyone?

Dream Machine

Healing Touch

RED LIGHT

A Hooker Who Loves Her Job

Complete Red Light Series Boxset

FREE - Through My Window - FREE

Star

Can't Buy Love

Free For All

PICK YOUR PLEASURES

Choose Your Own Adventure Romances!

Pick Your Pleasure

Pick Your Pleasure 2

RACING FOR LOVE

MMF Menages With Race-Car Driver Heroes

Complete Series Boxset

Driven

Shifting Gears

PARANORMALS

Vampires, Witches, And A Man Trapped In A Painting

Paranormal Double Pack Boxset

Picture Perfect

Reborn

PENTHOUSE PLEASURES

Naughty Manhattanite Neighbors Find Kinky Love

Taboo

Kinky

Sinner

Mentor

ROAMING WITH THE RYLONS

Non-fiction Travelogues about Jayne & Mr. Rylon's Adventures

Australia and New Zealand